"What Time Are You Free?"

he persisted.

"At about midnight, when I retire to my room," she said and rose.

"I'll go to the bar," David declared. "But I don't want you worrying all evening that you've driven me to drink, Lisa. It's true I wouldn't be on my way to guzzle Scotch if you were more sociable, but every man is responsible for his own soul. You won't worry about it, will you?" he asked with a serious face. Only the laughter in his eyes gave him away.

"I assure you, it won't cause me one moment's pang," Lisa informed him.

"That's what I was afraid of."

JOAN SMITH
has written many Regency romances but likes working with the greater freedom of contemporaries. She also enjoys mysteries and Gothics, collects Japanese porcelain, and is a passionate gardener. A native of Canada, she is the mother of three.

Dear Reader:

I'd like to take this opportunity to thank you for all your support and encouragement of Silhouette Romances.

Many of you write in regularly, telling us what you like best about Silhouette, which authors are your favorites. This is a tremendous help to us as we strive to publish the best contemporary romances possible.

All the romances from Silhouette Books are for you, so enjoy this book and the many stories to come.

Karen Solem
Editor-in-Chief
Silhouette Books

JOAN SMITH
Trouble in Paradise

Silhouette Romance

Published by Silhouette Books New York

America's Publisher of Contemporary Romance

SILHOUETTE BOOKS, a Division of Simon & Schuster, Inc.
1230 Avenue of the Americas, New York, N.Y. 10020

Distributed by Pocket Books

ISBN: 0-671-57315-2

First Silhouette Books printing August, 1984

10 9 8 7 6 5 4 3 2 1

Map by Ray Lundgren

America's Publisher of Contemporary Romance

Printed in the U.S.A.

BC91

Books by Joan Smith

Silhouette Romance

Next Year's Blonde #234
Caprice #255
From Now On #269
Chance of a Lifetime #288
Best of Enemies #302
Trouble in Paradise #315

Trouble in Paradise

PARADISE INN
(A Honeymoon Resort in the Pocono Mountains)
All places are fictitious.

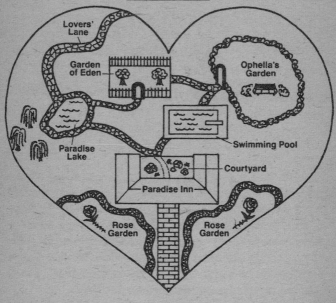

Chapter One

A breeze from the lake tousled Lisa's hair as she stared bemusedly into the water. The sun warmed her shoulders and transformed her Titian hair to a coppery halo. The first of June, she thought. It was a beautiful time for a wedding and apparently others thought the same thing, as Paradise Inn was nearly full of honeymooners. They strolled arm in arm along the cobblestone paths, and sat on benches, hands entwined, looking into each other's eyes.

Lisa had been surprised at first to see the number of hours honeymooners spent silently regarding each other, beyond words. What thoughts went through their heads as they sat endlessly gazing? Were they thinking of the past, of their first meeting, the proposal, the wedding? Or was it a contemplation of the future that beguiled them into those strange silences? Whatever it was, it invariably brought a misty smile to their faces. Lisa smiled, too. It was impor-

tant to her that all the honeymooners be ecstatically happy
during their brief stay at her inn.

She was quite unaware that while she watched the guests,
one of the guests watched her. When the Bertrams, a young
couple from New Jersey, strolled to the white wrought-iron
bench by the lake's edge and sat down, Lisa moved on. She
took a leisurely walk eastward toward Ophelia's Garden.
Her heart swelled with pride as she surveyed her domain.
Singlehandedly she had turned her late father's small family
inn in the Poconos into this enchanted oasis. It had been a
good investment of his insurance money; her only regret
was that he couldn't be here to see it.

The tall dark-haired man who had been watching her
stood irresolute a moment, then turned and followed her,
but at a slow pace, not trying to join her. Lisa stopped to admire the rose-covered arch that marked Ophelia's Garden.
The plants favored by Ophelia hadn't provided the lush atmosphere Lisa wanted, so she'd planted roses instead, eked
out each year with pink petunias, cosmos, and a border of
sweet alyssum. Everything here at the inn had to be lush
and romantic. Satisfied that it was, she entered the arch.

She sat on the bentwood bench, concealed by the hedge
all around, and listened for visitors. If anyone came through
the arch, she would leave. She heard a footstep, and
prepared to run off after a brief, friendly greeting.

The man who entered the garden was tall enough that he
had to duck his head. The first view she had of David
Spencer was the top of his black head, glinting in the sun.
Then he lifted his face and stared at her, as if surprised to
find a woman alone in this romantic spot. The eyes that
directed a startled, questioning look at her were deep,
ink-blue. She stared back a long moment, noticing his lean,
tanned face, the small creases that suddenly formed about

his lips as he smiled at her. Then he straightened his shoulders and she became aware of his height, a little over six feet, and of the width of those shoulders, tapering to a trim waist.

She peered over his shoulder for the inevitable bride. Men didn't travel unaccompanied through these connubial gardens. There was bound to be a bride in tow, unfortunately . . . but she didn't appear.

"You must be Ophelia," the man said, pointing behind him to the sign that topped the trellis arch. "You look more like Patience on her monument, smiling at grief. What's the matter? Did you and hubby have a tiff so soon?" he asked with a friendly smile.

His attitude was wrong. Young husbands here didn't take lovers' quarrels as a matter of amusement. His outfit was wrong, too, she noticed as he advanced toward her. He wore a navy cashmere sweater, open at the neck, with a blue shirt showing. His gray slacks and tan suede shoes were also wrong—elegantly casual. The bridegrooms usually arrived in their Sunday best, neither casual nor very elegant either.

"Not at all. I just work here," she replied briefly. The guests didn't care who owned the place, unless they had a complaint.

"Ah, that explains your unusual state of solitude," he said, walking around to look at the flowers. "I noticed the guests here go in pairs, like animals on Noah's ark. No, you wouldn't be Ophelia, or you'd be rooting out these trespassing roses and things that don't belong here. 'Rosemary, fennel, pansies, columbine, daisy'—I don't see one of them," he said, turning to smile over his shoulder. "Your employer can't be a lover of Shakespeare."

Not only handsome, but well informed. Her interest was

piqued. It was the first time she'd been taken to task for the wrong flowers in Ophelia's Garden. But then she already knew this man wasn't like her usual customers. He was a decade older, for one thing. It was the young newlyweds who liked her place, and the young weren't usually well off.

"And the violets withered all when my father died," she said, to show him she knew her *Hamlet,* too.

His brows lifted in surprise. They were sleek brows, as though drawn on by a charcoal pencil. "A lover of Shakespeare!" he exclaimed, and walked over to sit beside her on the small bench. All the benches at Paradise Inn were made for two. "Somehow I didn't expect that in this corny place," he said bluntly.

"If you find it corny, why are you here?" she asked, swift to take offense.

"It's a case of dire necessity. There's a convention on in town. This is the closest place I could get a room for the night."

"I see," she said, though she hadn't heard of any convention in Spelling. She wondered what accommodation he had taken. There were only two vacancies. The Romeo-and-Juliet room—he'd certainly find that corny, with the balcony and all. The other was the showpiece of the inn, the Imperial Suite she called it. Now that would really give him a laugh. The pink double tub shaped like a heart, the round bed, the hearts-and-flowers wallpaper. Okay, so it was corny, but the usual clients loved it.

"What entertainment does the place offer at night?" he asked, turning to regard her with interest. She was struck with the idea that he had come alone. Single customers *did* occasionally book in, usually travelers in a hurry to find a night's pillow. They seldom stayed more than one night when they realized what they had stumbled into.

"There's a dance after dinner," she told him. "The couples don't usually stay at it for long—" She came to a quick halt as he regarded her with a lazy smile.

"That's understandable. It *is* a honeymoon hotel after all," he said, as the smile stretched to a grin. She shifted uncomfortably under his penetrating gaze.

"Yes. Well, excuse me. I have to go now," she said, and stood up. "Good-bye, Mr. . . '."

"Spencer," he said. "David Spencer. I don't believe I caught your name either. I'm surprised it isn't emblazoned in a heart on your blouse," he said, peering down to see if he'd missed it.

"Lisa," she said, with another surge of annoyance at his attitude. But a customer was a customer, and she remained polite.

"*Miss* Lisa?" he asked, with a pointed look.

"Yes, Miss," she said, and walked swiftly from Ophelia's Garden.

Lisa entered the inn by the back door and went straight through to the lobby, where Lefty Spinner sat at the switchboard, reading a book. Lefty was quite possibly the most handsome man who had ever entered the doors of Paradise Inn, but that wasn't why Lisa had hired him. It hadn't been easy to find a social director who didn't object to cleaning the pool and cutting the lawn and doing any odd jobs that turned up—especially at the miniscule salary she could afford. Lefty did them all poorly, if he did them at all, but he had a friendly way with the customers, and he did *look* good at the desk and around the place.

His well-shaped golden head would be bleached to white by summer's end. His broad shoulders would be bronzed, and he would never appear in anything but white, to enhance his image. Perhaps it was his looks that gave him the idea he could coast through life, doing pretty well as he pleased.

Lisa glanced at the cover of the book he was reading. It had to do with reincarnation—so like Lefty, wasting his time.

"Hi, Boss Lady," he said, looking up with a smile in his topaz eyes. It was the compromise title, better than his original "Lisa Baby," but still less formal than she liked. "You have *got* to read this book," he told her. "Fantastic. It opens up new horizons—a whole new way of looking at life and death. I can hardly wait to die." This was a new tack. He more usually spent his spare moments inventing new definitions of life.

"Which room did Mr. Spencer book, Lefty?" she asked, hardly listening to his foolishness.

"The Imperial," he told her, with a sage nod. "There's a hundred bucks we didn't count on. He didn't blink an eye at the cost either. He's got a sweet little white Lotus parked outside."

"Why should he object to the price? He wouldn't get a suite at that price in a big hotel. Make sure he's got everything he needs, will you? Send Nancy up to check it out. I have to go to the kitchen."

"Will do," Lefty said with a wink, and plugged in the call for a housemaid at the old-fashioned board that still used wires and a headset.

Lisa went to the kitchen to speak to her chef to ensure that dinner was progressing smoothly. The pink bubbly wine from California was chilling, and the chicken breasts were simmering nicely in their sherry sauce. The salads were crisp and fresh, and the dessert—a rich concoction of sponge cake and fresh strawberries—was ready to be topped with pink whipped cream. Corny again, but cute, and good value for the money. Her *young* customers would appreciate every detail, but as the ink-blue eyes of Mr. Spencer lingered at the back of her mind, she wondered what that debonair gentleman would make of it.

If he disapproved, he could have a steak or bacon and eggs. Her menu was limited, but in the case of a violent dislike or an allergy, a few simple substitutions were possible. It was time to dress for the evening. Lisa ran quickly up the back stairs to her own apartment. She had a bedroom with bath, and a small living room. Her meals were taken downstairs, unless she had them sent up to her room, which she did occasionally.

The hearts and cupids and flowers of the rest of the inn were missing here. She'd kept the best of her parents' furniture and redone her set of rooms in a restrained, traditional style, an escape from the pervasive aura of romance.

After a quick shower, she prepared for the evening and brushed out her short coppery hair which feathered back from her brow. It framed a heart-shaped face, with a dusting of freckles across the bridge of her nose. It was the bane of her life that her pale complexion didn't tan, but flowered into freckles in the sun. Her eyes were her greatest asset—wide-spaced, and of a clear and pellucid green, fringed with thick lashes. The majority of her time now was spent in improving them. She applied eyeliner and a shading of green eyeshadow, with a silvery sheen for evening. Her cheeks didn't need rouge as they were flushed pink from her afternoons in the various gardens, but she applied a blush of shimmering color to her lips. Dismayed at the sulky expression she discovered on her face in the mirror, she smiled, revealing a row of straight white teeth, obtained at considerable cost and inconvenience from a set

of braces that had plagued her adolescense. She'd have to
do a lot of smiling before the night was over.

On Saturday, her busiest evening, she wore a white
scooped-neck blouse and long pink taffeta skirt that rustled
when she walked. The blouse set smoothly over the curve
of her bosoms, and around her waist she wore a wide sash
tie that emphasized her small waist, the feminine curve of
hips. Her aim wasn't to appear seductive but festive for her
paying guests.

The couples wanted to meet each other, and the best way
to do it was by organized affairs. There would be dances in
which partners were exchanged, spot dances with prizes of
a half bottle of the bubbly pink wine or a box of chocolates.
Lisa alternated the chores of M.C. with Lefty. It was never
wise to leave Lefty alone in charge of affairs. On Saturdays,
a trio of hired musicians played live music for the dance.
During the week, Lisa used records.

The evening entertainments were fun, or used to be. Was
five years too long at the same job? She examined the face
in the mirror again. The smile had faded, leaving a sad,
reflective expression behind. But she had nothing to be sad
about. Her turn would come; one day she'd be the bride,
and someone else would be the hostess. She was only
twenty-four—it wasn't as though she were ancient. Meanwhile, she was the proud owner of the inn, and if her plans
worked out, it would soon be a larger, fancier kind of
establishment.

She lifted her chin, squared her shoulders, and hastened
down the stairs to meet Leo Marshall. He had been her
dad's assistant and bookkeeper, and now he was hers. Leo
was a comfortable, sensible, unimaginative old bachelor
who was like a second father to her. He had a room on the
third floor, which he'd had for as long as she could

remember. A small advantage to keeping him on was that she didn't have to dine alone, amidst all the happy couples.

The dining room was full. Candlelight flickered on the glass and stainless steel, creating an illusion of crystal and silver. On each table a small bottle of wine sat in an ice-filled bucket. The bouquets looked handsome, with the artful arrangement of ribbon that could be used several times, but never once it began to grow ragged. She was economical, but not tacky. The couples, two at each table, filled the room with the buzz of young adults in a happy mood. Some of the bridegrooms were a little louder than was quite polite, but they were nervous. For the same reason, the brides giggled more than was seemly. Everything was as usual, except for the lone man in the corner with his black head bent over the menu.

"That's Mr. Spencer, the one who took the Imperial Suite," Lisa told Leo, who nodded with interest, peering over his shoulder. Leo lent the place a dignified note, with his silver hair and regal bearing. Despite his grand looks, he was the best handyman an inn ever had. If only Lefty would pitch in and carry his weight, things would be easier for Leo.

"I see he's refused the complimentary wine. That looks like a Scotch he's having," he said. It was the absence of fruit in the glass that gave this hint. The hotel's cocktails had fanciful names, and came trimmed with cherries and pineapple or slices of citrus fruit.

Mr. Spencer sat back in his chair, gazing around at the customers, with an expression of tolerant amusement. As he caught Lisa's eye, he nodded to her. He looked decidedly out of place here, so elegant and sophisticated he'd be more at home at the Ritz. She nodded and smiled back, then diverted her attention back to Leo.

"How did it go at the bank yesterday?" he asked, with a little frown of worry.

"We've been so busy I haven't had a chance to talk to you. Well, the man I spoke to—it was a Mr. Pender, the branch manager—said they'd consider the loan," she told him. "They want to see my books, of course, to find out how much profit we're making before they lend money for the expansion. I told him I've had to turn away customers. I could *easily* fill the extra ten rooms during the summer months, but he's a little leery about the rest of the year," she explained.

"Did you tell him we do a roaring business at Thanksgiving and New Year's and Valentine's?" Leo asked.

"Yes, and I pointed out that several of our clients come back for second and third honeymoons, too," she went on. "We've never actually *lost* money, even in the worst year, but of course summer and spring are our heavy seasons. I think we have a pretty good chance," she said.

"I don't see why not," he agreed.

"I want everything to be *perfect* when Mr. Pender comes on Monday, Leo. Thank goodness we're nearly filled up. He'll see how well I run a business, with your help. I think I'll take him on a tour of the place, with special emphasis on the Imperial Suite, the grandest one in the place."

"You've done wonders is all *I* can say," Leo congratulated her. "I thought you were a bit rash, investing all your dad's insurance money in renovations, but it's paid off handsomely."

"I was tempted to sell when that Everett woman wanted to buy the place and turn it into a health spa, but I'm glad I didn't. Dad used to tell me the only difference between men and women—in business, I mean—is that women ask whether they'll be *allowed* to do a thing, and men ask who can stop them. So I asked who could stop me, and decided no one could. They won't stop me now either, Leo,'' she continued, her voice firm, her eye decisive.

"My only regret is that you have to work so hard. Nobody'll try to stop you, if expanding is what you want to do," he said, and began eating his salad.

"If the Spelling bank turns me down, I'll just go to some other bank. I'm a good risk. I can do it," she said, and looked around at her customers with a proprietary air. They all looked happy, till she looked across the room to Mr. Spencer. He was picking at his chicken breast with his fork, digging in vain for truffles, perhaps, since the menu boasted them.

Later she noticed Mr. Spencer show his mirth with a wide smile when his dessert was served. She thought perhaps it was the sparkler adorning the top that amused him. Flambéed desserts were beyond her chef's talents, but it was simple to lower the lights and light a sparkler, and the guests usually loved it. When the lights were raised again, she saw him scrape off the whipped cream before devouring the fruit and sending off for another helping. The fresh strawberries *were* delicious, she noted with satisfaction.

While she was sipping her coffee, Lefty sauntered into the dining room, causing the brides' heads to turn. He certainly looked handsome, in his white linen suit. "I'll run along to the dance hall and see that everything's ready," he said, lifting the last strawberry from Leo's plate and popping it into his mouth. "I'll have to blow up some balloons. Angie Bey couldn't come in this afternoon. Toothache."

He noticed from the corner of his eye that the women

were looking at him, and struck a dramatic pose, reluctant to leave. "The world's a big balloon, when you think about it," he said.

"The right shape anyway," Leo agreed.

"I'm not talking *shape*, Leo," Lefty said, offended. "Bright, beautiful, but evanescent. One pinprick and it's gone." He shrugged his shoulders philosophically and sauntered out.

"He's a bit like a balloon himself. Full of hot air," Leo said, shaking his head. "I'm going to take a look at the faucets in the Romeo-and-Juliet room. There's a drip there that needs fixing."

"I'm just going to finish my coffee and join Lefty," Lisa said.

She leaned back to survey her domain with a feeling of accomplishment and satisfaction. Before she had examined two tables, Mr. Spencer was at her elbow, holding his coffee in his hand, and asking permission to join her.

"Sit down. I'd be happy for your company," she told him with a wary smile. He was here to poke more fun at her establishment; she knew it as surely as she knew his suit was tailor-made, and his silk tie matched his eyes beautifully.

"Was that the proprietor with you?" he asked in a conversational tone. "You've already told me you're single, so I'm not faced with fearing you've hatched a May-to-December match," he added, smiling.

"No, that was Leo Marshall, the assistant manager," she said, using Leo's official title.

"Does the Greek god type own the place?" he asked, obviously referring to Lefty. "Burnes, I believe the name outside says."

"Mr. Burnes passed on five years ago," Lisa told him,

still not admitting she was the owner. For the first time in her life, she felt a little embarrassed at her creation.

"A surfeit of pink bubbly, topped off with pink whipped cream, was the culprit, I expect," he said in his customary amused way.

"No, a heart attack was the cause, actually," she said curtly.

"Ah, then it would be the firecracker that did him in. It gave *me* quite a turn when it started shooting off in all directions, right under my nose. Fortunately I'm stout-hearted. I survived."

"So I see," she said, her tone chillier than before, though she realized Mr. Spencer had no idea it was her father he spoke of so lightly. "I hope everything was satisfactory in your room," she added to get away from the subject.

"Marvelous. I keep waiting for Cupid to pop out from behind a pink ruffle and shoot me dead," he told her. "With a pink arrow, naturally. I wonder if they consider the color an aphrodisiac."

"I don't believe those are required here," she answered, trying to control her temper.

"A *bizarre* place," he went on, seemingly unaware that he was annoying her. "I've stayed in *posadas* in Spain and on a *kibbutz* in Israel. I spent a summer with a family of farmers in France when I was in high school, and stayed two nights in a grass hut in Tahiti, but I've never come across anything quite like this," he told her, looking all around. "I'm surprised there aren't rose petals sprinkled on the floor. Such a nauseatingly singleminded pressure to mate. Do you know, even my *bathtub* is shaped like a heart!" he said, and laughed heartily.

"Yes, I do know it," she replied stiffly. "Most of our

guests are young honeymooners, as you can hardly help but notice.''

''Hardly!'' he agreed, with a rueful look around at them. ''But the sojourn is not a total loss. I've met *you*. You seem a fairly sane young woman.'' He sat back and examined her at his leisure, while a flush crept up from her neck. ''What time does the dancing begin?'' he asked suddenly.

''In one hour,'' she said, looking at her watch.

''Hmm, an hour to get in. What do most of your guests do in the interim? Now that *was* a foolish question!'' he exclaimed, and laughed. ''But as I didn't happen to bring a bride along with me, perhaps you can recommend a different pastime for us, Lisa.''

She ignored the hint that they should do something together and said, ''You'll find a TV set in your room, Mr. Spencer. The bar is also open.''

''It's such a lovely evening, I thought perhaps . . . Ophelia's Rose Garden . . . ?'' he suggested, with a little peek from the side of his eye for her reply.

''What a good idea! Why don't you go ahead? There's also a little lake and a Lovers' Lane,'' she told him blandly.

''I knew there'd be a Lovers' Lane!'' he exclaimed. A debonair laugh floated from his mouth. His white teeth flashed in the shadowy light from the candles. Even while Lisa's resentment of his attitude burned her, she was very much aware that he was extremely attractive. ''Shall we go out for a stroll? Walk off that heavy dinner?'' he asked.

''You forget I work here. I'm not free at the moment,'' she countered.

''What time *are* you free?'' he persisted.

''At about midnight, when I retire to my room, but don't let me keep *you* inside if you feel the need of exercise,'' she said, and rose.

"I'll go to the bar," he decided. He rose and drew her chair out, with no evidence of ill humor, but one black brow arched to show he was aware of her mood.

He accompanied her from the dining room, with a nonsensical flow of talk all the way. "I don't want you worrying all evening that you've driven me to drink, Lisa. It's true I wouldn't be on my way to the bar to guzzle Scotch if you were more sociable, but every man is responsible for the destiny of his own soul. You won't worry about it, will you?" he asked, with a serious face. Only the laughter in his eyes gave him away.

"I assure you, it won't cause me one moment's pang," she told him.

"That's what I was afraid of."

She left him and went to the dance hall to see how Lefty was progressing with the balloons. He was mopping his handsome brow when she entered.

"It's hot in here, Boss Lady. Next dough we get, let's put in air conditioning," he said.

"Open the windows, Lefty. Leo put the screens on a week ago." Air conditioning! She could hardly wait to have it installed. It was going to be part of her expansion.

Lefty began opening windows from one end of the long room, and Lisa began at the other. As they worked, Lefty called to her, "Who is this Spencer dude anyway? He's not our usual type of guest."

"I don't know anything about him," she said.

"Classy guy."

She ignored it completely. "Everything seems all right here. I'm going to my office and see if there are any messages."

"I'll go back to the switchboard. Did I tell you I used to be a pharaoh?" This amazing discovery, brought on by the

book he was reading, was gone into in some detail, but Lisa
had learned to close her ears to Lefty's wilder ramblings.
Her mind had reverted to David Spencer. Who was he? And
why was he showing so much interest in her? She really
hadn't said a civil word to him since his arrival, yet he
persisted in following her. Maybe it was time to be civil.
She didn't have many men like him throwing themselves at
her.

In her office, she had a dozen things to do—check
bookings, reservations, cancellations, orders for food and
laundry service. There was plenty to occupy her time, but
she spent half of that next hour staring out the window at an
ancient pine tree that towered over the hotel and groaned
menacingly in every storm. "A hazard," Leo called it, but
it was such a beautiful hazard she couldn't bear to cut it
down. She didn't notice the tree in particular that evening,
though. She kept thinking of David Spencer. Maybe she'd
have a few dances with him, if he went to the dance. One
disadvantage of turning her father's lodge into a honeymoon hotel was that all the men who came were very much
taken. And as her work occupied so much of her time, she
didn't get out to meet men. She hadn't missed it at first, but
lately . . .

It was the season—that was the trouble. With love and
romance all around her, she was bound to feel these
disturbing, lonesome sensations. Night was the worst time,
when all the happy, loving couples went upstairs together,
and she went alone. Well, she'd be alone tonight, too, but at
least she'd have a few dances with someone other than
Lefty or Leo. David would laugh at the "corny" pink
balloons, and she'd try not to take offense. Of course it *was*
corny, but the inn wasn't designed for world-weary sophis-
ticates. She'd ransacked her mind and a number of books

for every romantic cliché she could find, and the place looked it. But clichés weren't clichés unless they had meaning for a large number of people.

They had meaning for her, once. Five years ago, she hadn't found any of this corny. Maybe she'd grown up, matured since that time. Maybe she'd even outgrown her dream. She sometimes thought it would be more fun to run a small, exclusive inn: hire a really superb French chef, set the place up with antiques, have a squash court and tennis. But it would cost a fortune—out of the question. Time to come thumping back to reality.

Chapter Two

At five to nine, Lisa went to her room and put on fresh lipstick, brushed her hair, and tidied her clothing. The image in the mirror was no longer sulky or wistful. A light of anticipation flickered in her green eyes, and a smile lifted her lips. There were already about half the couples in the room when she arrived. They were beginning to drift together, making friends with each other, planning outings, and almost certainly discussing their weddings. Lefty wasn't around, so she went to the microphone and began her spiel, which was known by heart, worn smooth by repetition over the years.

"Good evening, and welcome to Paradise Inn. I hope you have a *wonderful* evening. We're here to help you." Familiarity with the words allowed her to observe the surroundings. She saw a drift of balloons around the edge of the room as she spoke. Lefty had blown them up too large.

They'd be popping like champagne corks all night. Darned Lefty, he was so unreliable. Pop! There, it had begun.

The first dance was designed to mix the couples up—at each tweet from the whistle, one couple changed partners with the couple on their right. She'd worried at first that the newlyweds wouldn't like to be apart, even for a moment, but it had proved untrue. They did like it; it seemed to add a certain piquance to their togetherness.

The next dance she left them alone, and the one after that would be a spot dance. It was during the spot dance that she saw David appear at the door. He entered and stood against the wall, with his arms folded, looking. She couldn't see his expression but she knew what it would be—amused tolerance.

When the normal dancing resumed, he strolled forward to greet her. "With luck, we may nab a bottle of the bubbly," he said, taking her hand without asking her to dance, simply assuming she would.

"Too late. We've missed the spot dance," she said, going into his arms.

"I'm sure there'll be other delights in store for us," he answered, folding her in his arms, while his dark eyes smiled into hers. "Mexican hat dances, square dances." But Lisa felt the greater delight would be just being with him. A faint aroma of spice and musk wafted from him, as he guided her gracefully around the floor.

"You mentioned you don't get off till midnight. What time do you begin work tomorrow?" he asked.

"Sevenish—it depends."

"Have you reported this to the authorities? They have laws against such abusive practices nowadays," he told her with a smile.

"I get plenty of breaks. I'm not exploited," she assured him.

"Do you like working here?"

"Very much."

"The hearts and flowers don't pall after a while?" he asked, feigning astonishment. She shook her head. "You must be one of those increasingly rare creatures, a romantic," he decided.

"Rare? The world is full of them!" she countered.

"No, the world is full of people who *call* themselves romantic. With women it seems to mean they like lace, and appreciate frequent gifts of flowers and other exotic trifles."

"And what does it mean to men?" she asked with interest.

"I believe the accepted definition is that they're willing to wait till the second or third date for reimbursement for the gifts," he answered sardonically.

"Isn't that rather cynical?" she asked, leaning back to look up at him.

"*I* make no claim to being a romantic. Of course, that's not the whole of it. Pretending to like poetry helps, and a maudlin sentimentality at the sight of brides and babies. Not simultaneously, it goes without saying," he added with a stern look.

"Where are you from, David?" she asked suddenly.

"An air of mystery is more romantic, don't you think?" was his evasive answer. "Think of me as a stranger in a strange land. We two strangers meet briefly in the vast sea of the universe," he said, with a psuedo-dramatic voice.

"Like ships that pass in the night, you mean?" she queried, refusing to feed his ego by inquiring further. Besides, she could check him out in the inn's register.

"I hope we do more than *pass*," he replied, tilting his

black head down to gaze intimately into her eyes. "I'm looking forward to a fine collision, say about twelve-fifteen, in Ophelia's Garden. There must be some local place open afterward that we could go to, to discuss the hazards of ocean voyages."

"I'm sure there is, but unfortunately my eyes close for business at about that time," she said.

For about two seconds he looked offended. Then a firmer expression settled on his mobile features. "There is a tide in the affairs of men, Lisa, and I'm sure Shakespeare would have included women, too, if it wouldn't have ruined his prosody—which, taken at the flood, leads on to fortune."

"Very true, but I don't see any fortune accruing to me as a result of one date," she pointed out.

"What price can be put on romance?" he asked, then answered himself. "A hundred bucks a night, if it's the Imperial Suite we're talking about, actually."

"The hotel provides only the setting," she said, pulling back as his grip tightened insensibly around her.

"My tongue stumbled on that one," he said quickly. "I wasn't suggesting anything lubricious. Please quell the urge to mention a Freudian slip. I, for one, don't hold with the theory that Freud knew everything. A drink in some civilized tavern was all I had in mind." He looked at her, waiting for an answer.

She wouldn't have minded going with him, but his evasiveness annoyed her. She'd dance with him a little longer, before deciding. "What do you do for a living, David?" she asked.

"How thoroughly pedestrian a question!" he exclaimed in mock dismay. "I'm disappointed in you. I was hoping you'd ask me whether I was a Libra or a Leo, what my favorite color is, whether I sleep in pajamas or the buff.

Meaningful questions, of the sort movie stars get asked," he said, gazing into her eyes, with a flicker of mischief lighting those inky pools.

"A lawyer, perhaps?" she guessed, noting his evasive tactics.

"I'm a Leo, actually. Favorite color is the sea-green of Grecian seas, to be seen north of the Aegean only at the Paradise Inn in Lisa's eyes, and then only till twelve-fifteen P.M., at which time they close for business."

"Pajamas or in the buff?" she asked, giving up on common sense.

"I was hoping you'd ask," he said with a very intimate smile. "But as the legal boys say, *quid pro quo*. You tell me your secrets, and I'll tell you mine."

"Fair enough. I'm an Aquarius, and my favorite color is black—as opposed to being in the red, you know. I think that's about as personal as I care to get with a stranger," she said with a bright, impersonal look.

"It'll do for a start," he said, unoffended. "And we're acquaintances now—this is our third meeting. We'll be fast friends in no time. And, incidentally, if you're in the red after slaving each day from sevenish till midnight, you require an accountant, or a lawyer. I should think the proprietor is making a good living here," he said, looking around. There was more than casual interest in that searching look, and the little frown on his forehead.

Another balloon chose that moment to pop. David looked behind him in alarm. "What do they call this dance? The heart attack waltz?" he asked, gulping.

The music ended, and Lisa excused herself to return to the microphone. When she looked around for David later, he was gone—just disappeared from the room. She concluded he'd gone off to some bar in town to pick up a woman, and forgot him, or tried to. But some pleasure had gone out of the evening. She was alone again, amidst all the happy couples. She should have gone out with him when he asked, without waiting till midnight. Lefty could take over the duties here as he'd often done before. She picked up a loose pink balloon and went to sit against the wall, watching the dancers.

"I've heard of a wallflower, but a wall *balloon*, Lisa?" David said, suddenly appearing from nowhere at her side. "How original, and courageous. It may blow up in your face at any moment," he cautioned.

"Oh, you're still here!" she exclaimed, with a smile lighting her face. "I thought you'd left." The pleasure was back.

"No, no. I'm hanging around, waiting for midnight, when we're scheduled to collide. I just had to make a phone call. You didn't think me cruel enough to leave you to the mercy of the loving couples?" he asked, taking up the chair beside her and reaching for the balloon she held. He rubbed it against his jacket to give it an electrical charge, and placed it above her on the wall.

"There's a full moon out tonight," he said, reaching to grasp her hand. "I peeked out the front door. It's fat and orange—well, yellowish. White, actually, but orange sounds more enticing. Not exactly fat and full either. Sort of gibbous and scrawny. A fingernail of white moon is what there is. Will you come out for a walk?" he asked with an enchanting smile.

"The truth will get you anywhere. You talked me into it," she said. "I'll just get Lefty to take over here."

"Is that the Apollo guarding the silent switchboard? The

fellow who's descended from the Egyptians? He doesn't look foreign, does he?'' David said, with a dubious little frown.

"No, he's changed complexion over the centuries,'' she said mysteriously.

"Are we talking reincarnation?'' David asked.

"Oh, yes. This week he's into reincarnation,'' she said, with a disparaging smile.

"Thank God!'' David exclaimed, with what sounded like genuine feeling. "I'm happy to learn he's a fool. I can handle competition, but a live-in Greek god is a bit much for me. I'll meet you at the door. I didn't get through to my party on the phone. The line was busy, so Lefty's trying again. I'll send him along here.''

With a last look at the couples, Lisa sighed happily. Lefty couldn't do much harm here alone for a while. Already heads were resting on shoulders. The couples were dancing more closely now. In a few minutes, they'd begin drifting off to their rooms to make love.

When Lefty came in, she asked him if David had completed his call. "Yeah, he got through to his mother,'' he told her. "She's from New York. I don't know if he lives at home or not. He's not very communicative,'' Lefty said, frowning. "I wouldn't be surprised if he used to be a cat of some kind—maybe a panther. There's a sly way about him, don't you think, Boss?''

"Maybe even *your* cat, Lefty. The pharaohs loved them,'' she said with a smile, and ran off.

"All set?'' she asked David, who was waiting at the front desk.

He gave her one of his debonair smiles that took place more in his eyes than on his lips. "Give me your hand, and I'll follow you anywhere,'' he said, taking her hand in his.

They went out into the still night air, with a crescent moon riding high in the sky. He tucked her arm in his and they struck off toward the lake.

"I hope I haven't upset you with my glib remarks," he said, inclining his head down to hers. "I'm not really a sour old realist, you know. I just didn't realize I'd stumbled into a love nest, and was a little surprised at the place. Actually, it's cleverly done." She was heartened at this faint praise.

"Thank you. It's done on a shoestring, too. Since you're making your confession, I've got one to make, too. I'm the proprietor," she told him. "All the bad taste you've been mocking is mine."

"I know, that's why I'm apologizing. It isn't bad taste if you believe in it," he said leniently.

"How did you find out?" she asked, surprised.

"Lefty told me just now. I'm really sorry if I sounded snide and condescending. I was just showing off, trying to impress you with my worldliness. I have one more confession to make. I never spent a single minute in a grass hut in Tahiti. I've never even been to Tahiti." She sensed that he was more sincere at this moment than he had been thus far, and liked him better for it.

"I forgive you. I don't even know exactly where Tahiti is," she admitted. "This is the pond that I call a lake," she said, with a little shrug of embarrassment.

"It's a beautiful lake. Things don't have to be big to be beautiful," he decided, after an examination of it.

"I had it dredged and put in the lily pads and frogs."

"Where'd you get the frogs?" he inquired with interest, real or pretended.

"The frogs were easy. Lefty and I caught them at a neighbor's pond." His interest made these trivial disclosures easy.

"I'm jealous of Lefty. I happen to be very good at catching frogs myself," he told her, with a boyish bid for approval.

"It was the darned lilies that kept dying on me. I had the sides of the pond landscaped with a rock garden over there," she told him, pointing across the water. "The willows were already there, but I put in the benches."

"I can't see them. When money allows, you should have it floodlit at night. It would look lovely," he said, looking all around.

"Yes, but it would cost a lot to have the electricity brought down here, and the lights installed. There are a couple of dozen apple trees over there," she went on, pointing to the east, "which we call the Garden of Eden."

"Appropriate. What would a paradise be without an apple tree to tempt Adam?"

"The trees yield, too," she continued, losing her sense of embarrassment as David became less mocking. "My chef makes a mouth-watering apple pie. Do you want to see the Garden of Eden?"

"I'd love to. Should we pluck a fig leaf before entering?" he asked archly.

"No, and you don't have to strip either. It's a modern Eden."

"Pity," he murmured, walking down a bricked path with her.

"It's really only about twenty yards away, but by curving the path, it makes a longer walk, and prettier," she pointed out. "Another arched trellis. Leo's handy at carpentry. He made them for me."

"A devoted employee. I don't have to be jealous of Leo, do I?" he asked, ducking his head under the arch.

"Only if you have aspirations of becoming my father. He

worked with my dad before I took over.'' David gave her an unfatherly grin.

As they strolled through the mini orchard, she found herself telling him her life story, in bits and pieces. "The lodge—it was called Paradise Lodge in Dad's time—was doing poorly," she told him. "We didn't have the facilities to draw in business travelers. There was no pool, no tennis courts, nothing like that. I added the pool with Dad's insurance money, and made a few improvements inside—or changes, if you don't consider them improvements," she modified.

"For a honeymoon hotel, let's stick with improvements," he decided. "Did you spend *all* your Dad's insurance money?"

"Every penny."

"You don't think it might have been wise to hold on to some emergency funds?" he asked, surprised.

"He wasn't insured for a million, David. It was hardly enough to do what I wanted. At the moment, I'm after the bank for a loan to expand," she added proudly.

"I think it's the right size now. Intimate," he said. "And if you expanded, your kitchen facilities wouldn't be large enough, nor the little dance room," he pointed out.

"This isn't a casual whim," she told him, her chin tilting up defensively. "I've got everything planned. The present bar will be annexed to enlarge the kitchen. They're adjacent. The dining room becomes the bar, the dance hall the dining room, and a new dance area will be built. It'll be a night club-*cum*-dance room."

"How about your pool, and all the gardens?" he continued, taking a real interest in her plans.

"The pool is plenty large—it was built with expansion in mind. Leo may have to build a few dividing walls for additional privacy in the gardens, but they're not the main attraction. The guests mostly use them for taking pictures.''

"I see," he said hesitantly, nodding his head. "You appear to have thought everything out. It's a lovely area—the Poconos all around, the river, too. How's business in the winter?" he asked suddenly.

"Dreadful," she admitted frankly.

"Couldn't the place be worked as a ski lodge in the winter, with all the hills around?" he asked, and looked sharply for her answer.

"None nearby is used for skiing. They're very densely wooded," she explained.

"Not that densely. It's half shrub," he pointed out.

"No, I'm a honeymoon haven, not a ski resort. Skiers would find the place corny, like you did. I don't plan to change its flavor," she said simply.

"You really *are* a romantic, Lisa," he said with a tsk-tsk. "You're losing out on a good business proposition."

"Maybe I am, but I'll stick with what I know. This is the end of Eden," she said, as the apple trees thinned out into meadow.

"We still haven't toured Lovers' Lane. Where is it?" he asked.

"It's back behind the lake. I have ten acres all told, but nearly half of that is between the main building and the main road."

"Have you any plans for developing it?" he asked immediately.

She was a little surprised at the extent of his interest in her business. "No, it's so pretty it would be a shame to destroy it with something tacky like a miniature golf course," she said.

"That *would* be tacky, but a restaurant or some facility to serve the general traffic, not related to the hotel, would make a good profit," he pointed out.

"My dad planted those rose bushes," she said, remembering the gardens that would supply her tables with fresh blooms in a few weeks. "He and Mom ran the lodge from the time they married. I couldn't bear to root those roses out."

"You could move them to the rear gardens," he persisted.

"They do very well where they are—the exposure and drainage suit them. No, I'm not that greedy. I won't move them," she said firmly.

They came out from the orchard and wended their way around the lake, over toward Lovers' Lane, a hedged-in walk bordered with lilacs. Her long skirt wasn't designed for walking, but the paths were well maintained, and it was only here in this area that her skirt was grabbed by the encroaching shrubs. It was shadowed and dark in the snaking path after they entered the lane. The crescent moon gave a pale light, but when Lisa felt her skirt being pulled, she had to stop and bend down to free it.

"That one holly bush will neither grow nor die," she complained, pulling herself loose from its sharp leaves.

They didn't resume their walk immediately. In a voice she mistrusted, David asked, "What's Lovers' Lane for, Lisa?"

"For walking in. Why do you ask?" she said, her suspicion rising.

"For *lovers* to walk in, you mean?"

"Yes, most of our guests are lovers," she agreed. "It's a very private spot." She was aware, there in the enveloping darkness, of its privacy. The scent of lilacs fading was heavy on the air. All day she had been feeling transient sensations of dissatisfaction at her single state. She'd been wondering what it would be like to be kissed by those debonair lips, and now she was going to find out. As sure as the moon was in the sky, David Spencer was going to kiss her. The sharp, spicy scent of his cologne blended with the lilacs as he inclined his head to hers, and she lifted her lips to his.

His lips stopped before touching hers. "You're prevaricating, young lady. Lovers' Lane is for making love in," he said softly, his breath fanning her cheek. "Is it effective?"

"Very," she murmured, waiting for the kiss.

"You've tested it out?" he continued, reaching his arms forward and placing his hands on her arms. She felt the warmth of his fingers beneath her thin blouse. His dark, shadowed face loomed above her, another pale moon.

"No, not like this," she said on a breathless whisper, as his lips claimed hers.

There was a muted fluttering of wings from the lilac bushes as some bird disapproved of the interruption. She closed her eyes and savored the luxury of the embrace. His lips moved softly against hers as he drew her against his chest, his hands splayed against her back. One hand slid down to encircle her waist, drawing her more tightly against his firm, masculine body. She raised her arms and looped them around his neck, returning his kiss.

It had been too long since she had done this. She was overreacting. Her pulse shouldn't be racing like a schoolgirl's on her first kiss. Her heart shouldn't be beating wildly, erratically, reverberating in her throat. She shouldn't feel this strangled desire to swoon in David's arms, only because he was kissing her in Lovers' Lane. Then his lips moved beneath hers, hardened, while his hands and arms increased their pressure, one hand reaching to the small of her back to press their hips together, there in the wan moonlight. Their hips, their thighs, pressed close, and without being aware that she did it, her fingers moved up his neck to play in his hair, enjoying the crisp, rough feel of it.

His lips opened, and his tongue pressed against her lips, moist, warm, demanding insistently. Her lips parted and she felt the exploratory thrust of his tongue within her mouth, caressing, engendering in her an indescribably yearning ache. His hands, on her lower back, slid lower, clutching her hip bones, pulling her against him. A slow heat grew in her, sending licking flames through her veins, robbing her of sane thought.

She'd stop in a minute, just one minute more of feeling his tongue work its magic within her, of that pulsing pressure that was growing deep inside her. How long would it be before this happened again? How long before a devastatingly attractive man wanted her as David did? A knot tightened in her stomach as his knee pressed between her thighs. Now. She must stop now, or she wouldn't have the strength to stop at all.

She held her breath and pushed him back, her hands clutching his shoulders. "David, stop," she said, her voice husky.

He looked at her with a wild, lost look in his eyes, or so the shadows made him appear. "You must be mad," he breathed, and pulled her back into his arms.

There was a rustle of branches behind them, the sharp click-clack of high heels on the paving stones, and a woman's voice called out. "David. Yoo-hoo! Are you here, darling? It's me, Marnie. They told me at the hotel you went out for a walk."

David pushed Lisa away with a sharp, rough motion. His

hands went automatically to his head to smooth his hair, then grabbed at his tie. "Here, Marnie," he called back in a calm, unruffled voice. "Miss Burnes was just giving me a tour of her place."

The click-clack hastened toward them, but already David was advancing to meet the woman—Marnie, who called him "darling." Lisa walked out behind him, her mind in a whirl. Beyond the shadows of the lilac hedge, she saw the woman, caught in a shaft of moonlight. She looked white and shimmery, almost ephemeral.

It was the cloud of pale hair and a white dress that created that strange illusion. Even by moonlight, Lisa could see Marnie was young and very beautiful. Her hair was softly curled and nestled just below her ears. A petulant sulk drew her lips into a pout.

"Well, introduce us, David," the woman said.

"Darling, this is Miss Burnes. Miss Burnes, my—"

"*Wife* is the word David is trying to say, Miss Burnes." Marnie finished the sentence for him, with a meaningful, knowing stare at David.

"How do you do, Mrs. Spencer?" Lisa said in a tone that tried to suppress her feelings. "I'm delighted to meet you."

"I bet you are," Marnie replied in a sarcastic tone, looking Lisa up and down. Then she turned back to David. "Shall we go, darling? I have such a lot to tell you. Sorry I was late. They told me at the desk you'd been trying to reach me. Did you think I wasn't going to make it?"

"No, no. I've been waiting—looking forward to your arrival," he assured her. "Excuse us, Miss Burnes. I'll see you in the morning. A very interesting place. Thank you so much for showing me around." His face was expressionless, but she had an impression of laughter in his voice.

"You're welcome, Mr. Spencer," she said with a chilly nod.

He already had hold of Marnie's arm to return to the inn. He looked back over his shoulder with a reckless wink. "We'll continue where we left off," he said.

"David, what on earth were you . . ." Marnie's voice died off in the distance, and Lisa was left alone at the mouth of Lovers' Lane, feeling a perfect fool.

Chapter Three

Lisa composed herself and returned to the inn five minutes behind the Spencers. Lefty stood near the switchboard, drinking a Coke.

"You might as well knock off, Lefty. There won't be any calls at this hour of the night," she told him.

"Did you get a load of Mrs. Spencer?" he asked, with a fondly foolish smile that told Lisa he was in love. Lefty's occasional crushes on her customers had caused trouble before.

"Yes, she's lovely," she said. "And *married*. Please remember that."

"Yeah, but she has eyes for old Lefty," he replied. Lefty had an annoying way of letting his head waggle loosely when he wished to be suave. It was wagging now. "And if I'm not mistaken, Boss Lady, Mr. Spencer isn't blind to your charms."

"We were just out back looking around. He seemed quite interested in the place," she explained casually.

"Who is this Spencer anyway? I mean, what does he do?" Lefty asked. "Did you weasel it out of him?"

"I have no idea. Some sort of businessman I suppose," she said. *And a very evasive one*, she added to herself. What was the big secret? "What's the address on their registration?" she asked, and pulled the book forward to read it for herself.

New York, N.Y. He'd registered with an American Express card, which gave only the name and number. Not very revealing. But what did it matter? He'd be leaving tomorrow with Mrs. Spencer, and that would be the end of it. What a despicable, underhanded person he was—and what a fool she'd been to fall into his arms at the drop of a hint. That phone call before they went to the garden was to learn his wife's probable hour of arrival. He was either misinformed, or he didn't care if his wife caught him with another woman in his arms. It doubtlessly wasn't the first time. She was about to go to her room when the switchboard lit up.

She took the call herself as Lefty waved good-bye. It was room nine, the Bertons. Mr. Berton was a little worried about his wife. She wasn't feeling well. *Oh, Lord, food poisoning!* was the first awful thought that flew into Lisa's head. The switchboard would be lit up like a Christmas tree if that were the case. Doctors, ambulances—and would it all be cleared up before the banker arrived on Monday? He'd be bound to hear rumors of it at least.

No, it wasn't quite that bad. Debbie had a rash and a fever, he thought. Should they call a doctor? Lisa encountered brides with nervous eczema about twice a year, and knew from the doctor's previous visits that it was a psychosomatic thing, bridal night jitters. Doc Abbott would only give her a tranquilizer and perhaps a little fatherly talk, but on the off chance that it was measles or chicken pox, she offered to call the doctor.

This delayed her own sleep, as she waited till Doc came downstairs with his black bag before she left the lobby.

"Same old thing," he told her, with a little laugh. "We're seeing less of it nowadays, I must say. The girl was as nervous as a kitten, and the groom not much better off. She's settling down fine now. I don't think you'll hear from them again."

"I'm sorry to call you out at this hour, but I didn't want to take any chances. I diagnosed the problem, but the A.M.A. wouldn't approve of an innkeeper's prescribing drugs," she explained apologetically.

"I suggest you prescribe a shot of whiskey the next time," he told her, then left.

Lisa didn't have a rash, but she felt nervous, too, and prescribed a piña colada for herself, just before the bar closed down. The last two couples were leaving the dance hall. That was one good thing about her sort of establishment. The guests retired early. Soon they'd all be tucked into their wedding beds, two by two . . . including David and Marnie, though this wasn't their honeymoon.

She took her drink up to her room and mused about their relationship while she sipped. She decided they'd been married for three or four years. David was a chronic strayer from the path of fidelity, and Marnie accepted it for reasons of her own. She wasn't above giving the eye to other men herself, if Lefty told the truth. The Spencers were a very poor advertisement for marriage, and she was sorry they had come to her honeymoon hotel to disillusion her newlyweds. What would they think if they had seen David with her in Lovers' Lane, kissing her as if he meant it, then saw his wife with him the next day?

From her window, she had a view across the courtyard of the windows in the Imperial Suite. The lights were still on, casting a rosy glow through the drapes. So David and Marnie weren't in bed yet. He was probably getting the tongue-lashing he deserved. While Lisa sat watching from her darkened window, the lights switched out. She felt an ache in her breast, a gnawing pain at being left out in the cold—again. What she needed was a holiday—a change, a rest. How long was it since she'd gone anywhere? Five years, and she couldn't possibly go this season either with the busy wedding months ahead, and along with that her expansion.

She settled her mood by concentrating on the expansion, and when she went to bed half an hour later, she managed to sleep.

Morning was busy with some breakfasts to be served in bed, others in the dining room. Debbie Berton had recovered from her rash and came downstairs, wearing an enviable glow of fulfillment. Lisa was alert to see how the Spencers behaved together, but was disappointed. They had breakfast in their room and sent down for a second pot of coffee. A leisurely meal, then. No hard feelings between them after the previous night's fiasco. Later, she saw them strolling together those same paths David had strolled with her the night before.

Lisa was required to reestimate the length of their marriage. They didn't hold hands, touch, or smile fondly; neither did they seem to be estranged. They acted like old friends. They must have been married a long time, long enough for passion to have died, and bland acceptance to have set in. It was hard to understand how David could be immune to his beautiful wife. She was lithe and long-limbed, with all the exposed parts of her body toasted golden brown. The white sundress she wore set it off beautifully. Even the new bridegrooms gave her a second look.

Lisa made a determined effort to stay out of their direct path. When the coast was clear, she went to the front garden to gather flowers for the tables. She wore a scowl as she snipped and placed the cut blooms in her basket. She didn't hear David walk up behind her, and she jumped in surprise when he spoke.

"Is the pool open for swimming yet?" he asked, after a polite greeting. She saw over his shoulder that Marnie lagged behind, observing another part of the garden.

"The heater's been turned on, but it's still a little cool," she said, forcing herself to give a civil reply. "If you can stand seventy degrees or so, you can swim. It's up to you."

"Seventy degrees will seem warm after this chilly shoulder you're showing me," he said in a quiet voice, with one of his dashing smiles.

"What time were you planning to leave, Mr. Spencer?" she said, with no warming of her attitude. "Check-out time is twelve-thirty."

"Leave?" he asked, astonished. "We're not leaving today. We plan to stay a few days. It's all set with the pharaoh. He told me the room wasn't booked till next Saturday."

Her heart sank. "What do you want to stay here for?" she asked, chagrined.

"I'm a little tired. I want a quiet holiday. I've come to appreciate the romantic ambience here," he added, with a long look across the garden to Marnie. Lefty had joined her. The wagging of his head told Lisa he was being suave, making a fool of himself over Mrs. Spencer. She was struck at the same moment at what a truly beautiful pair these two golden people made.

"I can conduct some of my business affairs from here by phone," David added, drawing her back to business.

"It's up to you," she said brusquely, reminding herself of the nightly room fee, and the bar tab, which she could certainly use. A silver peal of laughter came from Marnie's direction, as she smiled flirtatiously at Lefty. "I'd like you both to realize, however, that *business* affairs are the only affairs to be conducted," Lisa added primly.

"I can stand it," he replied laconically, with a rueful glance at the laughing couple.

"I wish you could stand it with a better grace!" she snipped, her patience giving way. "You're like a specter at the feast, smirking at my other guests. There are lots of hotels in Spelling. Why don't you stay somewhere else?"

"I'll tell you a little secret," he said, leaning down till his head nearly touched hers. "I'm smitten with the innkeeper at this spot. Glorious sea-green eyes, she has. You wouldn't think a green sea could spit sparks, would you? An incredible phenomenon," he said softly, gazing into her eyes.

"If you don't want to see her spit something else, I suggest you leave her alone," she said, and cut off a bud that wouldn't be open for a week.

"You were wishing that was some part of *me* you could just cut off and kill, weren't you?" he asked, smiling with pleasure at this whimsy. "I suppose you're a little upset about last night."

"No, I'm more than a little upset."

"I didn't think Marnie would be arriving before today," he said shamelessly.

"You wouldn't want to waste a night! It's despicable that there should be a Marnie to arrive—*ever,* after the way you behaved," she said indignantly.

"I couldn't agree with you more, but we can't very well get rid of her. Surely you're not suggesting . . . murder!" he said, in mock horror.

"Oh, I think you're insane!" she exclaimed.

"No, just a little light-headed," he said blandly. "What you don't understand is that we have an . . . uh . . . *open* marriage. More of a business relationship than anything else," he said, in a little confusion.

"How nice. And have you shared the secret of what this mysterious business is with her, or does she consider it more romantic to remain in the dark?" Lisa asked with a bold stare.

"She knows," David said, with a wicked smile that told her he knew she was fishing to find out herself, and that he had no intention of obliging her.

There was another burst of laughter across the garden. David turned toward its source and Marnie called to him. "I don't believe it. Bleeding hearts!" She laughed, picking a flower.

A pair of strolling honeymooners were trying to pose for pictures beside the roses, but they moved away, looking at Marnie askance. She and Lefty walked across to join David and Lisa.

"The little thing hanging out is supposed to be a drop of blood," Lefty explained.

"How macabre!" Marnie said with a shudder of revulsion. "You told me it was *bad,* David, but you didn't say *how* bad," she said to her husband.

"I didn't say *bad,* dear. I said different," David corrected, without glancing at Lisa, though she thought he spoke for her benefit. "The roses are lovely, aren't they? A perfect exposure, as Miss Burnes was saying," he continued, ill at ease.

"Life's a garden when you think about it," Lefty decreed, going into a semi-trance that indicated a bout of philosophy. "Some of us are born in the sun and flourish into roses. Others grow in the shade—dandelions."

"There's a new twist for the horticultural world to consider," David said, looking in bewilderment at the speaker. "I wonder what would happen if you transferred a dandelion to the sun."

"You know what he *means!*" Marnie said, with an annoyed look at David. "Some of us are born with all the advantages, and others have to struggle. That's a deep thought, Lefty."

"They come to me," he said modestly, but Lisa wished he wouldn't feel obliged to share them with her guests.

The honeymooners who wanted to take photographs lingered at the edge of the garden, while Marnie continued with more laughing mockery of the inn. It was a relief when she said to David, "Now come and show me Lovers' Lane," in accents that revealed her interest was purely in being amused.

Lisa kept an eye on the Spencers from various discreet locations after they went behind the inn. She saw, though she was too far away to hear, that the older couple was disturbing her regular guests. Wherever the former went, and they went everywhere, the other couples moved away.

Paradise Inn wove a fragile spell over its clients. All it took to break the spell was one nonbeliever, and a pair was twice as bad. To make it worse, at lunch Marnie headed to a table with the Bertons. She kept up a bright stream of talk and laughter throughout the meal, but the Bertons were not amused. They wanted to be alone or with their own kind. Lisa noticed they were ill at ease, eating little. Soon Marnie began flirting with the new bridegroom, while the bride looked on, close to tears.

Lisa determined the Spencers would not remain another day, whether they had a reservation or not. They were ruining the honeymoons. She had to get rid of them before Monday, when the banker came to assess her business. It was the final straw when Mr. Berton cornered her at the desk and asked if he could get a refund for the rest of the week. His wife didn't quite like Paradise Inn, he said, blushing.

"I'm sorry to hear it," she said, feeling genuine sympathy for the boy, and he was no more than a handsome boy. Why couldn't Marnie leave him alone? She already had David and Lefty.

"It's not the place, Miss Burnes," he said earnestly. "It's a real nice place. It's that Spencer woman. She said she'd see us at dinner, and Debbie—well, she doesn't feel at home with a person like that."

Lisa suggested he find a reservation elsewhere, but knew he wouldn't find so many extras at the price he could afford. "The Spencers will be leaving tomorrow," she added. "I can arrange that they not join you for dinner, if that would help."

"I'll talk it over with the Moores," he said. "They were thinking of leaving with us. We're both from the same town. We got married the same day. I'll see what Ed says.

Maybe if we can have them at our table again, Debbie will feel better about staying.'' He was unhappy, but determined to please Debbie.

''I'll make sure you and the Moores dine together,'' she said. And she'd make sure the Spencers did not dine or sleep or anything else here after tonight.

She called Nancy, her upstairs maid, and spoke to her. ''I want you to remove all the towels from the Imperial Suite. Strip the bed of linen, and turn the heat up high.''

''What for?'' Nancy asked, blinking in shock. ''It's already too warm upstairs, Miss Burnes. Has she been complaining about things? That Mrs. Spencer is a pain in the neck.''

''No, Nancy, I'm the one who's complaining about them. I'm going to get rid of that pair if it kills me,'' she said firmly.

''Aren't they married?'' Nancy asked, eyes alight with curiosity.

''Of course they're married! Why do you say that?'' Lisa asked.

''I had the idea Mr. Spencer spent the night on the sofa,'' she said. ''When I took up their breakfast, he was on the sofa with a blanket over him, and she was in bed. They don't . . . *act* married,'' she said with a frown.

''They're not newlyweds,'' Lisa told her. ''They're past the stage of gazing at each other all day long.''

''But are they past sleeping together, too? They're such a handsome couple, aren't they?''

''Yes, very attractive,'' Lisa said curtly.

''Lefty says she invited him to look her up in New York. Can you *imagine?* She better be careful—he'll do it.'' She ran off with a chuckle.

Lisa pondered other methods to get rid of the Spencers.

She'd serve them cold dinner and warm drinks. Of course, she'd have to give them towels and linen eventually, but they'd have to send for it three times before they got it. She'd remove the soap, too, and anything else that wasn't nailed down. Drapes—strip the window and let the sun shine in on them at six A.M. She ran upstairs after Nancy to tend to these details.

"I'll tell them the draperies were sent out for cleaning," she said, unhooking them and folding them neatly, to hide in her own apartment. The cleaners weren't even open on Sunday, but she didn't care.

She also instructed Lefty, who had to be let in on the secret, that if the Spencers asked for a different room, none was available.

"You're crazy, Boss Lady," he said, staring with incredulous eyes. "It sounds illegal to me. Jeez!"

"Life's a battle, Lefty. I have not begun to fight!" Lisa told him, with an excited laugh.

"You're trying to botch my campaign with Marnie, right? Afraid of losing old Lefty. You heard she invited me to New York?"

"Every man for himself. Don't you *dare* let them have the Romeo-and-Juliet room!"

"Couldn't if I wanted to. Didn't you know the tap isn't fixed? It wasn't the washers after all. The whole faucet is out. Leo's got to pick up a new set. Oh, and did I happen to mention the freezer is acting funny? Herb's afraid it's packing up on us."

She heard this litany of woes in silence. "One catastrophe at a time. First get rid of the Spencers."

"You're the boss, but I still say you're crazy."

The changes to the Imperial Suite were made easier when the Spencers went off for a drive in the afternoon. They

were absent for over three hours, which gave Lisa time to
instruct her chef regarding the preparation of their dinner.
The toughest cuts of meat, left to cool on their plates before
serving, the most jaded salad, an added dash of malt
vinegar in their salad dressing, and day-old rolls. Before the
unsuspecting Spencers returned, the whole staff were in on
the trick. They had not only permission but encouragement
to be as unhelpful as possible.

It went against the grain for Lisa to treat paying guests so
badly, but she would *not* allow one couple to ruin the
honeymoons of the others, and to kill her chance of a loan in
the bargain. What would Mr. Pender think if he saw her
guests lined up with their cases, checking out early, and
complaining about the place? He wouldn't lend her a cent.
If she also had a private score to settle with David, there
was no need to tell her employees that detail.

The Spencers' response to her campaign was noticed
precisely two minutes after they returned to their room. Lisa
was stationed at the switchboard to listen in on the conversation. She had Mrs. Latham, an older woman who worked
year round, replace Lefty at the switchboard. There was no
counting on his discretion. It was Marnie Spencer who laid
the first complaint.

"There seems to be some misunderstanding about our
reservation," she said, in a voice showing a little impatience. "Our room has been totally stripped. We're not
leaving today."

Mrs. Latham, biting back a smile, explained that the
drapes were out for cleaning.

"This is ridiculous! Preposterous! What kind of an inn is
this?" she asked, the voice rising a pitch.

"A honeymoon inn, ma'am," Mrs. Latham answered
sweetly.

"Well, for God's sake, tell Miss Burnes to get something up on these windows for the night. I don't intend to undress in public. And we need towels, too, and soap. I want to take a shower immediately. Send them right up," she ordered angrily.

"Yes, ma'am," Mrs. Latham said, and hung up the receiver. "I guess they haven't looked under the bedspread yet to see their sheets are missing." She laughed.

"That's good. I'd like to keep that for a surprise when they're nice and tired," Lisa said with a wicked grin.

"Shall I send up the towels?"

"Oh, no, not yet," Lisa said. "We'll let her make a few more calls before we oblige her. I'm going to the bar to remind Lefty to hide the Scotch. Now remember, let her call two more times before you send up the towels. And make sure Nancy forgets the soap. That'll require another call."

"You'll never see the Spencers here again, or any of their friends either," Mrs. Latham warned.

"That's the general idea!" Lisa answered cheerfully.

By the time Lisa returned from the bar, Mrs. Spencer was placing her third call for soap and towels. Her cultured accents had become strident. "Are you sending up those towels, or must I go downstairs in my underwear and get them myself?" she demanded, no longer feeling it necessary to identify herself.

"Why, I sent them up ages ago, ma'am. Nancy must have got lost," Mrs. Latham said.

"Lost somewhere in the maze of two corridors! How ingenious!"

"I'll send someone to look for her," Mrs. Latham replied, and unplugged the switchboard cord.

"Remember, no soap," Lisa said and walked away, with just one niggling worry about the place's reputation.

No more was heard from the Spencers till dinner time, when Marnie strode purposefully to Lisa's table. She wore a different white dress, this one with large black polka dots, and a very full skirt. Sandals with narrow black patent straps called attention to her tanned legs. She looked ravishing, as usual. David was a step behind her, looking more bored than anything else. There were two vacant chairs at Lisa's table, but she didn't invite them to sit down. She noted with satisfaction that the Bertons and Moores were together again, but keeping a wary eye on Marnie.

After a stilted greeting, Marnie laid her complaints out in a polite but loud and firm way. She explained about the soap and towels, but it was the window draperies that concerned her now.

"What are you going to do about them?" she asked sharply.

"I'm having them dry-cleaned," Lisa said calmly. "I must apologize for their dusty condition earlier. The room wasn't rented, and it seemed a good time to arrange for cleaning."

"Even dusty drapes would be preferable to none. When you rented the suite at a hundred dollars a night, did it not occur to you to postpone the cleaning?" Marnie asked with a haughty stare.

"Why, no, it didn't," Lisa said blandly, with a peep at David, who was biting his underlip, and examining her with narrowed eyes. She couldn't figure out whether he was angry or trying not to smile.

"What are you going to do about it?" was Marnie's next question.

"The cleaners are closed now—what a shame! I'll call them first thing Monday morning and ask them to hurry. I don't see why a simple cleaning job should take a week, do you, Leo?" Lisa said, and took a sip of her wine, while Marnie held her temper, her chest heaving with the effort. "Was there anything else, Mrs. Spencer?"

"I want you to hang something on those windows this evening. I don't care if it's a sheet or blanket."

"Do we have a spare sheet or blanket, Leo?" she asked, but answered herself, in case Leo lost his nerve. "Do you know, I don't have a spare one in the whole place. The blankets are out for cleaning as well, and the sheets are at the laundry."

She was no longer in doubt as to David's reaction. It was a smile he was biting back. His flashing eyes gave the secret away.

"Let's not make a fuss about it, s-sweetheart," he said, with a little stumble on the last word. He placed his arm lovingly around Marnie's waist. "We can undress in the dark. It will be romantic. I'm surprised Miss Burnes hasn't stripped all the windows of drapes, to make it necessary for her other guests."

"I don't see why you put up with this treatment, David," Marnie said, frowning at him.

"The conference in Spelling is over today. You might find a room in town now," Lisa suggested artlessly.

"Oh, no, not when you're putting yourself to so much trouble to make us comfortable. Sending everything out to be cleaned—that was thoughtful of you. With such treatment, we may remain indefinitely," he told her, with a triumphant twinkle.

"Oh, no, *we* will not," Marnie told him. "*You* stay if

you feel you must. *I've* seen quite enough of how this place is run.'' She turned and flounced away to sit at a table not assigned to her, with one of the honeymoon couples.

"Your wife is at the wrong table. I've put on place cards," Lisa told David.

"Need I ask which is ours?" he inquired, looking around the room. "No, I needn't. I see you've thoughtfully put us right outside the kitchen door. We'll enjoy the pleasant domestic clatter of pots and pans and the friendly passing of the waiters. The added heat will be welcome, too. We wouldn't want to catch a chill, after the way you've warmed our room up for us." His bland manner turned to a kindling glare. "But if you've directed the waiter to pour soup on my head, Lisa, be prepared to take the consequences.''

"Why didn't I think of that!" she exclaimed, smiling.

"I can't imagine. You thought of everything else," he answered, and marched after Marnie to take up his chair by the kitchen door.

"He's certainly a good-natured lad. I was afraid he might be angry," Leo said.

Lisa watched the table and its occupants during dinner. She observed David refuse the wine with a batting of his hand. She also saw a surprised expression settle on his face, which she assumed was a reaction to learning the Scotch was gone. He questioned the waiter for a few minutes, at the end of which time the waiter departed and returned with two glasses of sherry. She added sherry to her list of things to be concealed.

When the two dinner plates were returned to the kitchen, Lisa nodded with satisfaction. On more than one occasion, she intercepted a baleful glance from David. Marnie's back was to her, but she got a view of the woman's pouting profile several times when various waiters bumped her chair. Finally Marnie had her chair moved to the other side of the table so that she sat at right angles to David.

Mrs. Spencer had taken the course of ignoring Lisa, but she and David seemed on excellent terms. They smiled and talked more amiably than before, almost as though to show the hostess they were enjoying themselves despite her efforts. They didn't eat much dinner, but they remained at the table till the bitter end. When Lisa and Leo arose to leave, the Spencers followed them out.

They're going to tell me they're leaving, she thought, without any of the triumph she had expected to feel. She was almost sorry to think the escapade was over, that she'd never see David's laughing dark eyes again.

"Would you be kind enough to extend our compliments to the chef, Miss Burnes?" David said with a mocking smile. "A lovely dinner."

Her green eyes flew wide open, and her lips parted. "What?" she gasped.

"See you at the dance," he added, and hastened on to catch up with his wife.

"I don't believe it!" she exclaimed to Leo. "I was sure this would get rid of them." She tried unsuccessfully to frown.

"They're persistent," he said, worried. "Too persistent. I have a feeling there's something going on here that we don't know about. I had a little chat with Mr. Spencer after he returned from their outing this afternoon. He asked a lot of questions—*knowing* questions," he added.

"What do you mean? What kind of questions?" she asked sharply.

"Almost professional questions. He knows more than a little about inns and hotels," Leo said thoughtfully.

Lisa remembered her long conversation with him the night before, and had to agree that he not only knew about the business, but had been at pains to learn about her establishment in particular. She and Leo discussed what his reason could be for staying here after their rough treatment, and even for being here in the first place. An economy inn was clearly not their normal accommodation while traveling, and on top of that it was a honeymoon inn.

"Maybe he's heard you're trying to get a loan, and has taken the notion you're in financial trouble. He might be out to buy you cheap," Leo said. "I'm sure he's in the hotel business."

"I've got to get rid of them before the banker comes on Monday!" Lisa exclaimed. "They're just trying to make me look bad so I won't get my loan."

"Don't worry your head," Leo said consolingly. "You're not in debt, so a refusal on the loan won't force you to sell, if *that's* what he thinks."

"That's true," she said with a wave of relief. But she was still determined to be rid of them.

Everything must be perfect when Mr. Pender from the bank came on Monday. She would not allow a couple of spoiled city slickers to make her establishment look bad. She had worked too hard to fail now, and especially she would not permit the Spencers to be the cause of failing. Whatever it took to get rid of them, she'd grit her teeth and do it.

Chapter Four

David Spencer did attend the dance, but Lisa refused to dance with him. She was curious to discover what his wife was doing, as she wasn't with him. At the end of the spot dance, she went to wait near the door for her next duty as mistress of ceremonies. Lefty was supposed to replace her, but he hadn't shown up. There was a distinct possibility that he was with Marnie, which added to her concern. David strolled over and sat beside her. She stared straight ahead, ignoring him.

"I wonder if Leo would care to dance with me," he said, looking around the room for Leo.

"Does Mrs. Spencer not dance?" she asked, still looking ahead, though she had a very clear vision in her mind of the sardonic man who sat beside her, drumming his fingers on his knees to denote his ennui.

"I don't know. I never asked her," was his unexpected reply.

Her head spun toward him, shock on every line of her face, but she refused to question this unusual statement. She knew he was up to something, had some foolish joke he wished to utter.

"In any case, I expect she'll be too tired to dance by the time she gets her bed made up and the newspapers taped to the windows," he added blandly.

"Why don't you leave?" she finally asked.

"Because you're so very eager for me to. You've aroused my curiosity, Lisa—along with a few other instincts," he added mischievously, trailing his eyes over her body.

"You know you don't belong here. I don't want to be rude, David, but . . ."

"Yes, you do," he interrupted cheerfully. "You take great pleasure in discommoding me. It's a strange way for an innkeeper to behave, I *must* say." He gave her an intense, measuring look.

"You can't possibly be enjoying yourself," she pointed out reasonably.

"I haven't enjoyed myself so much since Marnie took a world cruise last year—*alone*," he said, with some meaningful emphasis on the last word.

"I don't blame her!" Lisa exclaimed in vexation. "The only wonder is that she ever bothered to come back."

His reaction to this was negligible. When he spoke again, he leaned his head down to hers and said in an intimate voice, "Will you tell me something, Lisa?"

"What?" she asked.

"Where did you hide the Scotch? There was a full bottle at the bar last night. The bridegrooms aren't drinking it. You wouldn't be a secret tippler, would you, sneaking the bottle up to your room?" he suggested playfully.

"Certainly not!"

"If it's really gone, I have a suggestion. When you get around to replacing it, change brands. Scotch should taste woody, but it shouldn't be made from resin," he told her.

"I never had any complaints before."

"You're getting a complaint now. A good hostess endeavors to please her clients," he pointed out. "You pleased so well before."

"That depends on the client," she said, with a disapproving stare, but it was hard to disapprove of this handsome adversary.

"I have your most expensive suite, and you treat me like a pariah," he complained.

"What point are you trying to make by staying here? You haven't done anything but laugh at my inn and put it down since the minute you arrived. The place is not for everyone, I grant you, so why stay?" She listened closely, giving him a chance to hint at his true motive, looking forward to telling him she wasn't in debt, if that was his hope.

"When I'm pushed, I have the obstinate habit of digging in my heels and shoving back. That's all," he said with a carefree shrug.

"I thought perhaps you liked the place so much you wanted to acquire permanent rights to it," she said, trying to lead him into an admission.

"No, no, it's not the *place* that intrigues me that much," he disagreed, leaving her to interpret by the glow in his eyes that she was the only attraction.

"If it's the hope of getting a dance with Leo that holds you, you're wasting your time. He doesn't dance," she said with a bored look.

He just smiled and shook his head. "Did it disturb you so much that a man found you attractive, that he wanted to kiss you?'' he asked, gazing fondly at her. "In fact, that he *still* wants to, very much?"

She felt a sensation of melting inside her, and a foolish thrill of pleasure, swiftly followed by disgust with herself. "I was not disturbed," she said, but in an overwrought voice.

"No?" he asked doubtfully, but interpreted the matter to his own satisfaction. "Then I'm making good headway. You're disturbed now. You get two charming splotches of pink just *here* when you're upset," he told her, touching the tops of her cheeks, rubbing the pad of his index finger gently over them. She knew very well the pink was heightening to red. She wanted to make some very clever and cutting reply, but no words came into her mind. She just gazed at him as he smiled softly at her.

"I . . . I'm not *disturbed*, just impatient with you," she said in a breathless tone.

"Then we have something in common. *I'm* becoming impatient, too," he told her gently. "I give you fair warning, Lisa, I plan to stick around. You have ample time to lay your plans. Shortsheet the bed, burn the morning toast, chill the coffee, but I shall remain—for better or for worse, for richer or for poorer." He stopped suddenly and emitted a light laugh. "I think that's how the ceremony goes—something like that." He looked surprised that he had slipped into reciting the marriage vows.

"Does that come before or after the vow of fidelity to the spouse?" she asked sweetly. "*I've* never been married, you see, and haven't had the experience of saying those words to anyone."

"Why, to tell the truth, I wasn't paying much attention at Marnie's wedding," he answered, unfazed. "What we were actually discussing was my determination to remain here."

She considered this remark and decided to be as calm as he was. "I'm delighted you're enjoying your visit at Paradise Inn, Mr. Spencer. Naturally, I'll do everything in my power to make your stay pleasant. I can use the money."

"I know," he answered, then rose and sauntered from the room.

Shortly after, Lefty came to replace her. "It's about time. Where have you been?" she asked, venting her anger on Lefty to relieve the tension.

"Trying to calm Marnie down," he said. "I had to turn down the heat in her room, Boss Lady. I nearly died of it myself when I was helping her cover the windows. We used tablecloths. If you're short tomorrow, don't blame me. She was running from door to door upstairs, disturbing the newlyweds at their play, asking them if they were hot. Some of them misunderstood. They think she's nuts. She's a bit spoiled, I think. Well, rich and beautiful and with a rich husband—it figures she would be."

"Maybe I'd better go to the switchboard. She'll probably be calling down," Lisa said, then went to the lobby. Perhaps this had gone far enough. The Spencers might be less troublesome if she treated them with a little extra consideration of the right sort.

Mrs. Spencer didn't phone, but she came storming down the stairs in person, clad in a black lace nightie and matching peignoir that reeked of Paris. A pair of regular guests were just passing through and stared at her, then hurried away, chattering about what they had seen.

"What is it, Mrs. Spencer? What's the matter now?" Lisa asked, all her good resolves dissolving.

"Do you really have to ask?" the woman said boldly. "My room is full of flies and mosquitoes. It was so hot I had to open the window. And where is David?"

Lisa ignored the first complaint, judging the latter to be what had brought her downstairs in this outfit. "You might try the bar. Mr. Spencer seems fond of his Scotch. And would you mind putting on some clothes before you do it? This is a reputable inn," she added, with a scathing examination of the black lace nightie.

"Is *that* what you call it, *reputable?*" A theatrical laugh hung on the air. "I've never been in such a disreputable, badly run hotel in my entire life. India was *nothing* compared to this! At least the servants weren't impertinent!" She continued a long, loud litany, and unless Lisa was very much mistaken, she enjoyed every minute of it. Marnie Spencer had a real flair for melodrama.

"I'm sorry. You caught us at a bad time," Lisa apologized. She had seen the heads hanging over the banister as the other guests gathered to enjoy the show.

"Obviously not even you could run an hotel so badly on a regular basis, or you wouldn't have any clients whatsoever. I give you warning, Miss Burnes, if there is *one more incident* I shall leave first thing in the morning."

Lisa was delighted to hear it. She eased Mrs. Spencer back up the stairs, telling her she'd send someone to look for her husband. Then all she had to do was come up with one more incident, and she'd be rid of the Spencers. It was difficult to create an incident after everyone had gone to bed, but she wanted to be absolutely certain the Spencers would check out early in the morning, before Mr. Pender from the bank arrived, so she sat cudgeling her brains.

A noise, a ruckus to interrupt them at, say, two-thirty in the morning, when they would be sure to be asleep. But

then to disturb only the Spencers and not the others would
be difficult. She was already on the verge of losing the
Bertons and Moores, who were remaining only on the
understanding that the Spencers would be leaving. She
thought of pebbles thrown at their window, a call from the
switchboard, but wasn't sure Marnie would consider such
details an incident. She also preferred that the incident have
no air of her involvement in it, as using the switchboard
would do. Something anonymous and annoying, and limited to the Imperial Suite.

It was at ten to twelve that she got her inspiration, and she
dressed in her oldest jeans and a fleecy jersey to carry it out.
One couldn't go into the dusty basement in a long pink skirt
and good white blouse. Tapping the pipes was the inspiration she had come up with. It would be easy to do, as new
plumbing had been installed to service the pink heart-
shaped tub. The copper piping still had a new sheen to it
which would make identification certain.

Lisa read in her room till two, at which time all sounds
had ceased along the corridors. She took a wrench from
Leo's toolbox in the kitchen and unlocked the door to the
basement. It was an old building, built in the days before
basements had concrete floors. The earth floor had a musty,
damp feel to it, and the lone light bulb hanging on a wire,
unshaded, gave off only a puddle of illumination, not
reaching to the pipes in the corner. She felt her flesh creep
as she tiptoed past the lighted area, into the darkness
beyond, where cobwebs and spiders lurked. Every slight
creak of timbers and groan of the trees beyond the high
windows was magnified. You never knew about these old
cellars. One window was ajar—someone could have
climbed in and could be crouching by the furnace to attack

her. Her heart hammered against her ribs, but the faint flicker of the new copper pipes beckoned her onward.

She lifted the wrench and began tapping the pipe, giving it measured knocks for about forty-five seconds. Then she stopped; after, she repeated it three times. This done, she scooted up to the switchboard to wait for the reaction. In fact, she didn't have to wait at all. The light from the Imperial Suite was glowing when she got there. She took the call. It was David.

"There seems to be something wrong with the plumbing," he said, his voice irritated.

"This is Mr. Spencer calling?" Lisa asked quietly.

"Lisa, is that you? What are you doing at the switchboard at this hour?" he asked. "Don't you *ever* get any rest?"

"What seems to be the trouble?" she said.

"There's an *infernal* racket in the bathroom pipes. It's intermittent, sounds as if a mad drummer had got loose in the cellar. Maybe you could shut off the water till morning. You won't be needing any water before then," he suggested.

"I'll see what I can do. Sorry for the bother. Was Mrs. Spencer disturbed?" she asked with keen interest—and total insincerity.

"I don't think so. She isn't stirring."

"Oh, good. Well, sorry."

"That's quite all right. I expected some revenge," he said, his voice dulcet. "I take it I can go back to sleep now? And you can, too. Sleep tight, Lisa." He hung up gently. She could not see him, but she had a vivid image of the amused smile he wore.

She returned immediately to the basement to bang on the

pipes. She did as before, tapping, then stopping, but the taps were more violent now. Marnie was a sound sleeper, it seemed, and it was Marnie who must be awakened. The stops were just long enough to give her listeners a hope the noise had stopped, before starting again. It was a horrible thing to do to innocent customers, but then the Spencers weren't really innocent. And Marnie had made a threat, which Lisa considered more in the nature of a promise, that she'd leave if there was one more incident, so the tapping went on.

The first fear of the darkness had dissipated. Intent on her job, Lisa didn't hear the soft approach of slippered feet creeping up behind her. The first intimation she had that she was not alone was the appearance of a shadow, suddenly looming before her on the wall. She saw it from the corner of her eye and gasped, while her heart skipped a beat. She saw her own moving arm stop in shadow, before she realized she was frozen immobile. A strangled scream, as weak as an infant's, pierced the air as the shadow moved menacingly closer. She was too petrified to respond, to take evasive action. Anything seemed possible there in the dark, isolated cellar.

"Well, well, what an odd time for a musical solo," David said, his voice echoing strangely in the empty room. At the sound of his voice, she was able to turn. She saw his hand moving toward hers to remove the wrench from her fingers.

"Oh, David, you scared me half to death!" she exclaimed, clutching her heart. Her fingers shook and her breath was uneven.

He hefted the wrench, regarding her with a menacing look. "You know what I ought to do with this, don't you?"

he asked with a fleeting glance to her head, as though
selecting the point of attack.

"I was just . . . just . . ." No inspiration came to her.

"I know what you were doing. The tapping was clearly
audible, as I happened to be sleeping in the tub," he told
her.

"The tub?"

A slow smile moved across his lips. "You heard me."

"But why on earth . . ."

"We're digressing. I'd like to hear your explanation for
this latest caprice," he said and folded his arms to stare
down at her.

"The pipes!" she said, pointing to them. "I was . . .
trying to repair them so they wouldn't keep you awake,"
she said and unwisely beamed a wide smile at her clever-
ness at coming up with this idea.

"Banging on a pipe with a wrench doesn't fix it, Lisa.
Even you must know that much about plumbing." He
turned toward the stairs. She hung behind uncertainly,
waiting for him to leave with her wrench, but as he flicked
the light off at the bottom of the stairs, she quickly
scampered forward, out of the darkness to follow him
upstairs.

"I want a drink of Scotch, and I want it now," he
ordered when they reached the landing into the kitchen.

"I don't know where Lefty hid it," she admitted.

"Then it *was* done on purpose, a deliberate campaign,"
he charged, watching her warily.

"You knew it was. Don't think Paradise Inn usually
serves tough roast beef and wilted salad, because it
doesn't."

"I knew the meal had deteriorated sharply from the night

before, but till one has eaten in a restaurant three times, it's not fair to judge the quality. We're going to the bar to look for that Scotch,'' he said and waited with the wrench in his hand till she went before him, looking nervously over her shoulder in case he might still decide to use it.

In the bar, David set down the wrench and began rooting through cupboards. ''This has been an extremely childish display you've put on for us,'' he said accusingly. But when he found the Scotch, a smile broke and he lifted it to the bar. ''Want some?'' he offered.

''No, thanks. I don't know how anyone can drink it. It tastes like turpentine.''

''I agree your brand does, but it's preferable to that carbonated, acidic beverage you call wine,'' he said, tilting himself out two fingers of the Scotch.

''How would you know? You never tried it. You always sent the bottle away unopened. You're paying for it anyway. A half bottle is included in the price of dinner,'' she told him with a superior smile.

''I'd gladly pay *not* to drink it. And, incidentally, I'm flattered to learn you've been watching me so closely.'' He sipped the much-maligned drink with every appearance of pleasure. ''Do you want anything here?'' he asked, plopping two ice cubes into his drink.

''Maybe I'll have a soda,'' she decided. ''It's a little warm.'' She didn't question why she was staying here with him, but knew she didn't want to leave, to go back alone to her room.

''You call this warm? You should have been in our room earlier, before we found the temperature gauge. I didn't think to look for it in a cupid's navel. Then there are the mosquitoes that breed so wonderfully in your stagnant pond,'' he added with a blighting stare.

"The man who usually sprays the area didn't come around this year. Is your wife still asleep?" she asked, deeming it wise to keep that woman in mind, because in spite of his complaints, David Spencer apparently still intended to remain as her unwanted guest.

"I trust she is. I kept the bathroom door closed to muffle the noise of the pipes," he said, his expression softening to something like a smile as he drank his Scotch.

She pulled the tab of her drink and didn't bother with a glass. "She promised she'd leave tomorrow morning if there was another incident. That's why I did it," she said simply.

"She has to leave tomorrow in any case. She has to be in New York tomorrow for work."

"Will you be going, too?" she asked hesitantly, not looking at him, but past him to the mirror of the bar. She didn't want to meet his eyes. When he didn't answer, she finally turned to look at him.

He was gazing at her with an intent, unblinking gaze. She felt warm from the soft expression he wore. "Perhaps," he said, sounding indifferent, but there wasn't indifference on his face. "I have to leave soon, in any case."

She felt a little shadow pass over her heart. The Spencers had been extremely troublesome guests, but it would be duller without them. None of her young newlyweds had been so interesting. She especially regretted to see David go, she confessed to herself. Why couldn't he have been a bachelor? He obviously wasn't in love with his wife anyway, any more than she was in love with him. Why did the most attractive man who'd ever stayed at the inn have to be married?

"Now, aren't you sorry for the way you've treated me?" he asked, adopting a conciliatory attitude. There was flirtation in those dark eyes, and on the lips that opened to reveal an edge of white teeth.

She noticed his hair, unkempt for once, giving him a youthful air, with one lock hanging on his forehead. She wanted to run her hands through it. His elegant dressing gown of camel's hair was loosely closed at the waist, with brown silk pajamas beneath.

"You deserved it," she said grumpily when she noticed the silence was stretching between them.

"Perhaps I did," he agreed easily. "You're not at all what I expected when I came here."

"Why should you expect me to be like anything in particular? We'd never met before," she pointed out.

"No, but hotels aren't often run by beautiful young women, with eyes like yours and hair like a flame," he said softly. As he spoke, his eyes lingered dreamily on the items mentioned. When he set down his glass, she took a step backward. She knew he was going to kiss her. If he touched her once, she wouldn't be able to stop that kiss, so she backed away, beyond reach. He followed, advancing as she retreated. There was a very purposeful air about him.

"I have to go now," she said. "Will you . . . will you turn out the lights when you leave?"

"What are you afraid of, Lisa?" he asked, stopping just two feet from her. He reached out and took the can from her fingers, looking at her all the while. "What do you think I'm going to do, right here in your own inn? One squawk from you would bring Leo or Lefty running."

"It's getting late," she said vaguely. She wanted to leave, to look away at least, but his gaze held her.

"It's nearly morning. It hardly seems worth while going back to my tub," he said.

"There's no one in the Romeo-and-Juliet room, if you were *really* sleeping in the tub," she offered.

"About all Marnie and I share is the name," he said, then took a drink of her soda. "I was in the tub, and I'll have the sore bones tomorrow to prove it. Marnie and I are . . ." He stopped with a cautious look, just on the verge of explanation.

"Getting a divorce?" she prodded helpfully. Surely that was it. Anyone could see there was no love left in their marriage, and he hadn't seemed a bit jealous of Lefty, who was positively drooling over the woman.

"No, no," he answered quickly, while her spirits sank.

"I'll get the key for the other room," she said, her voice curt, dismissive.

"Lisa!" He began to move toward her. It was David who looked disturbed now. "I should have told you why I'm here," he said with a guilty look.

"You don't have to tell me. I'm not a fool," she shot back angrily. "I have a pretty good idea why you're here, but you're wasting your time. I'm not broke, and I don't plan to sell. You've wasted your weekend and mine. I'll leave the key on the desk. Don't forget to turn out the lights."

"I won't. And thanks, Lisa," he said softly. He blew her a kiss just before she hurried from the room, as though the hounds of hell were after her.

She felt as if they were. If she didn't put some distance and doors between herself and David Spencer, she'd do something very, very foolish. Maybe she already had. Wasn't it foolish to fall in love with a married man who had no intention of divorcing his wife?

Chapter Five

Lisa dressed carefully for her interview with Mr. Pender in the morning. She chose a mint-green linen dress, crisp and tailored, that set off her green eyes and coppery hair. The smudges from lack of sleep under her eyes were hardly noticeable. Excitement overcame fatigue as she prepared for the visit. Lefty was hunched over the switchboard when she came from the dining room.

"Hi, Boss Lady. This is the big day, kid," he said, reminding her of the interview to come. "Don't sweat it. Life's a bus stop. If you don't catch this one, there'll be another along soon. Maybe you'll like its destination better," he told her, then looked back to his book.

"Were there any important calls?" she asked him.

"Marnie Spencer called down."

The blood in Lisa's veins turned cold. "What did she want?" she asked in a voice of doom.

"She'll be leaving at nine. I offered to bring down her bags."

"Thank God for that!" Lisa exclaimed with relief.

"You're welcome, Boss Lady," he said, intending no humor or heresy.

"Is Mr. Spencer also leaving?" she asked casually.

"She didn't say so, but I think she said something about his settling up her bill," he said over his shoulder.

"Yes, of course he would," Lisa replied, trying not to show her joy that David was remaining longer.

She went along to her office to see that the accounts and records were ready for Mr. Pender. Leo came to the door and asked if she wanted him to be there for the interview.

"It might be better if you're free to handle any problems that arise during the visit. Just make sure all the couples are properly looked after, and avert any disaster that looks imminent," she said nervously. "Mrs. Spencer may be checking out around that time," she added with a meaningful look.

"Let's hope she gets out before they come. Are you giving them a tour? You mentioned their real estate man might be coming along."

"I'll show them the Imperial Suite if Spencer is out, and one of the other rooms, whatever one is made up and vacant," she said, rubbing her hands nervously. "Oh, Leo, I hope they say yes. It means so much to me."

He looked at her worried face and tried to reassure her. "Why wouldn't they? You've done a good job."

"Yes, I guess I have," she said, but since meeting the Spencers, she was less certain of it. What if Mr. Pender thought the place was a joke in poor taste, as Marnie did? Would he lend thousands of dollars to expand a joke? But it was the balance sheet he was interested in. He wasn't here to judge her taste.

The Spencers had their breakfast sent up to their room again. By the time Marnie called Lefty up to help her with her bags, Lisa had died a thousand deaths, hoping she'd be gone before Pender arrived. She expected the woman's departure would be clamorous and unpleasant, but Mrs. Spencer was in a good mood, laughing with Lefty, and even asking where Miss Burnes was. Lisa quietly pushed her door closed to avoid being seen.

She heard Marnie giving Lefty her card and asking him to be *sure* to call her when he came to New York. "We'll have a ball. I'll show you all my spots," she promised. "You won't forget now?" Her voice fairly throbbed with sensuality.

"Lefty and elephants never forget" was his effort at being suave.

It was nine-thirty, half an hour to go. Lefty came into her office, of course without knocking.

"Hi, Boss," he said, his head wagging. "She's gone. I got her packed off for you."

"Thanks, Lefty," Lisa said distractedly. "Now, if you could just get Mr. Spencer out of his room, too, I could show it to Pender without any problem. Would you mind asking . . ."

"It's done," Lefty told her. "Dave's just left, too, in his own car. Coming back soon, he said. That Marnie's some chick. Tipped me a Jackson," he said, flashing a twenty-dollar bill.

"That was generous of her!" Lisa said, impressed.

"Class," he said, throwing up his hands. "Oh, by the way, she showed me some pictures of her kid. Did you know they had a kid?" he asked.

"No, I didn't know that," she said, trying to show only a polite interest, but her curiosity was rampant. "Boy or girl?" she asked.

"A real cute girl, named Cathy. She's three. She had a lot of pictures of them all together. Cathy has Marnie's coloring, and Dave's eyes. Kids are the crazy glue of marriage," he added, his eyes rolling ceilingward as they sometimes did when he was soaring into philosophy. "They hold it together when it's falling apart. That marriage is badly rent," he added sadly.

A child—how was it she'd never thought of that? In her imaginings, it had always been just David and Marnie, no longer in love, but a child added a whole new dimension to the matter. It shook her more than she liked to acknowledge, but this was no time to think of it. "It's no concern of ours," she said, wanting to get rid of Lefty.

"It might be of interest to *me*," he said with a wise look. "But what the heck—I like kids. Of course, she might not get custody, being an actress," he added.

"An actress!" That shouldn't have come as a surprise. The woman had always behaved in a theatrical way.

"Off Broadway. She's playing a carrot in an existentialist play translated from the French. *Tossed Salad,* it's called," Lefty continued. "She said they need a cucumber. Theirs is pregnant. They don't mind if a man takes the part. It's a speaking part," he added grandly. "Life's a bit of a tossed salad, when you get right down to it."

What could Lisa say to an announcement like this? "That's nice," she said uncertainly.

"It's a very serious play," he said, finding Lisa's reaction tepid. "All about how people have to learn to live in harmony with nature."

Lefty liked to talk, but this morning Lisa hadn't time to

indulge him. "I'm a little busy this morning," she said impatiently.

"Okay, Boss Lady. I just thought I'd warn you, you might be losing old Lefty. You'd better train up one of the girls to handle the switchboard." He strolled back to the lobby. Lisa looked after him, wondering that such a handsome head should hold such an insignificant mind. She didn't know whether she'd be glad or sorry to lose Lefty, but she didn't think it likely in any case. He usually gave these threats a couple of times a year. Last year he had had designs to go to Europe and become an *au pair* boy for a French couple, but nothing came of it.

She went over her outline for the banker while she waited for him to arrive. At ten o'clock on the dot, Lefty rang her office. "They're here," he said. "I just sent them in. Good luck, Boss Lady. You'll never guess who—"

She'd already hung up. This was no time for more of Lefty's foolishness. A nervous spasm gripped her as the fateful moment approached. She arose and went to her office door, waited ten seconds, then opened it. Mr. Pender, the high-domed, bespectacled man she'd spoken to at the bank, greeted her with a smile, but she only noticed this from the corner of her eye. Behind him walked David Spencer, with a bland smile on his face, and a laughing light in his eyes.

"I'm afraid this is a private meeting, Mr. Spencer," she said stiffly. "If you have any problem, Mr. Marshall will look after you."

"I have no problem," he said calmly and continued his way into her office.

"Of course you two know each other," Mr. Pender said, looking from one to the other. "Mr. Spencer is on the

Board of Directors of our bank. He's taken a special interest in this case."

Lisa was aware of the blood draining from her head, leaving her with a dizzy feeling and a humming in her ears. Surely she'd heard wrong! This impossible situation couldn't be real. It was one of David's little jokes, or a scene from Lefty's existentialist play. She couldn't have spent the weekend alienating the man who had to approve her loan! That's why he was here! What other "special interest" could he have?

"We're old friends by now, Ed," David said and smiled at her. It was a strange smile—not quite victorious, not jeering, but somehow . . . *friendly,* almost conspiratorial. "Miss Burnes has shown me all around the place, so you won't have to spend your time on a tour. Shall we all sit down and have a look at the books? I waited till you came to do that," he told Pender.

"Yes, of course, the books," Lisa said, striving to sound rational. The books—on her desk. *Walk to the desk. Don't faint, it's not businesslike. I'll kill David Spencer the minute Mr. Pender leaves—except that David will leave with him. I'll never see him again. Oh, God!* "We'll need another chair. I'll call . . ."

"There are three chairs here. I'll get the other," David said and walked across the room, where a wooden armchair stood against the wall.

The three chairs were arranged around the desk and they sat down together to go over the accounts. Assets, liabilities, revenues, debits, and credits were discussed for an hour, with frequent references to the columns of figures in her accounting records. Mr. Pender had a hand calculator, which he often used to make computations of his own. But

Lisa realized within fifteen minutes that it was an exercise in futility. She also realized that it was David Spencer who had the final say. Pender deferred to him in the manner of an underling, but it was Pender who was quick to point out the flaws in her operation.

"What you have here, Miss Burnes, is a borderline business," he said, regarding her dubiously. "It's self-exploiting. The only reason it works at all is that you yourself put in more than twelve hours a day, and take out of the operation a much lower salary than you'd make if you worked eight hours a day for someone else. In effect, you're underpaying yourself. It's simply not worth your while, financially speaking."

She considered this a moment and said, *"I'm* willing to do the work. *I'm* willing to take the low salary. I don't need much, since I live here."

"That is just my overall, general impression," Pender said. "We can go into more detail if you like. There are your employees, for instance. Are they willing to work such long hours for so little pay?"

"They're mostly college students. I have only a few year-round employees," she pointed out.

"Yes, I see here a Mr. Marshall, who is about at retirement age. Naturally, you'll have to provide some retirement pension for him, since he's been with the inn since your father's time. Then he'll have to be replaced as well, and you won't find a man to accept his job at his salary," he told her, peering over the top of his glasses.

She was stopped a moment at the mention of a retirement fund for Leo, but had some hazy notion that he'd just retire here, at his own room, at very little cost. "I expect Mr. Spinner will take over when Mr. Marshall retires," she said. But Lefty had often mentioned leaving. One of these days, he'd do it.

"He's a young man. He'll expect to make a career of the job, and be recompensed accordingly. Quite apart from the disservice you're doing yourself, you must see you're not dealing quite fairly with these gentlemen," Pender continued persuasively. "Then there's the matter of your actual cash position. To be perfectly blunt, Miss Burnes, you have none. No emergency fund whatsoever. What if you should have a claim laid by a customer? You're not even insured against public liability to any significant degree. Your revenues barely cover expenses. The smallest unforeseen calamity and you'd be in trouble."

"Miss Burnes is very inventive in dealing with unforeseen calamities, Ed," David told him, with a secret smile at Lisa over his head.

"Yes, quite, but you said yourself, Mr. Spencer, that we shouldn't risk a loan on the operation," Pender reminded him, rather huffily. Lisa cast an accusing look at David.

"That's true, I did," David agreed easily. "I can't see that the added revenue from new rooms would match the loan payments, but the situation is by no means desperate. Miss Burnes doesn't owe a penny. There's no present debt to worry about," he pointed out, looking at the books with sharp interest. Lisa regarded him hopefully. Was he going to suggest a *smaller* loan? She mentally trimmed her expansion from ten new rooms to five.

"I suggest you sell the inn. It's a desirable location," David said.

"To you, Mr. Spencer?" Lisa asked, her voice thin with anger. Leo was right, then. That's why he was here, to try to buy her out cheaply.

"I'm interested in it," he admitted warily.

"So I've noticed, but my inn is not for sale," she said firmly.

"Don't you even want to hear the price Mr. Spencer is willing to pay?" Mr. Pender asked, astonished at her attitude. He went on to tell her, whether she was interested or not. She was impressed by the figure. The offer from the woman who wanted to build a health spa had been much lower, but she really had no interest at all in selling. She'd never even thought of it, and certainly if she did sell, it wouldn't be to David Spencer, who had come here under false pretenses and caused her so much trouble.

Her interest was piqued at the offer, and she decided to question David about it. "Since you don't think *I* can run the inn profitably, how do you plan to do it, Mr. Spencer?" she asked with a thinly veiled sneer. "You would turn the front area into some profitable venture, I presume? You mentioned my waste of land in the rose garden. What did you have in mind? A hamburger stand?"

"No, and not a mini golf course either. I don't think it would be compatible with what I have in mind," he answered, unoffended.

"But Mr. Spencer has no intention of running the inn!" Pender interjected impatiently. "It is only the *land* he wants. There are plenty of other spots that can be picked up as cheaply, Miss Burnes. We're not trying to take advantage of you in any way. I personally feel the other side of Cobbler's Mountain would be preferable for what he has in mind."

"And what is it you have in mind?" Lisa asked, turning to David.

"We discussed it a little one evening. I'm going to build a ski resort in the Poconos," he told her. "I like Cobbler's

Mountain for various reasons—its height, and the fact that it's not too heavily wooded, and easily accessible. I can build here on your side, or on the other side of the mountain. I made this my first choice, as the service roads are already in and it's a little closer to Spelling. Of course, Paradise Inn would have to be torn down, and that—''

''Yes, I dare say that would cost as much as putting in your road,'' Pender continued for him.

''Oh, no. Paradise Inn is not being torn down,'' Lisa said calmly. She kept the turmoil within her own breast. How calmly these two men sat there, discussing the destruction of her life—the inn where she was born and grew up, and where she now made her living.

''It's a wonderful opportunity for you to get out from under,'' David said, as though doing her a favor.

''I don't want to get out from under! I'm not *under*,'' she hastily corrected. A cold anger clutched her heart, and her temper rose swiftly. ''I don't happen to be in debt. That must have come as a disappointment to you. You came here only to look my operation over and see how hard you could push me,'' she said accusingly. ''That's why you and your wife were running everything down, making fun of it, trying to upset my customers so they'd leave, and give my place a bad name. I think you're *despicable!*'' she said, her breast heaving. She got up from the desk, forgetful of Mr. Pender.

''What's this? *Wife?* Mr. Spencer, I had no idea you had got married!'' Pender exclaimed. ''May I be the first to offer my congratulations!'' He put out his hand to give David's hand a shake.

David pulled away from him, looking from him to Lisa with a worried, confused frown. ''No!'' he said to Mr. Pender, who let out a spontaneous huff of indignation. ''I mean—I'll explain later, Ed. I'd like to have a word with Miss Burnes in private, if you don't mind. Why don't you go talk to Mr. Marshall about—about . . .'' He stopped, ransacking his mind for an excuse to get rid of Mr. Pender.

"Yes, I'll do that, Mr. Spencer," Pender said obligingly and left, with David hastening him to the door.

David stood at the door, closed it quietly, and approached Lisa. Her face was set in anger. "This isn't what you think at all," he said warily.

"Isn't it?" she asked stiffly.

"I didn't come here to pull your place apart or try to squeeze your price down," he said firmly. "I admit I had my eye on your inn as a good building site, and I came here to look it over firsthand, but that has nothing to do with not giving you the building loan. If the inn had been a viable operation, we'd have given you the loan and looked elsewhere for our site," he told her with a worried, sincere face.

She listened with a part of her brain, but another part of it kept jumping back to Pender's surprised exclamation—"I had no idea you had got married!" But when she spoke, she didn't reveal her thoughts in that direction.

"It *is* a viable operation," she said firmly. "I've run it for several years, and my father did the same for more than twenty years before that. Don't think I'm going to hand it over on a platter because you want to put up a ski lodge. Not everybody in the world is as demanding and sophisticated as you. I have plenty of satisfied customers. I'll go on catering to people with less jaded appetites."

"Lisa, it won't work," he said, shaking his head. "You're teetering on the brink of financial disaster. Sell out while you've got a good offer; I'm prepared to be generous. I want to *help* you. You can start in some other line of business. I suggest something less labor intensive. An inn is all work. You know this place is running you ragged, working from dawn to past dark, and barely keeping your head above water." A commiserating look was in his eyes as he spoke now.

"Don't lay the sympathy on so thick," she suggested with a disdainful lift of her brow. "I'm not a slave, and I'm not starving to death."

Not quite, she added silently to herself. Not starving, but certainly run ragged, working too long, too hard. And for what? Not to have her life's work snatched out from under her on the whim of this conniving, arrogant developer!

"I have no sympathy for a stubborn woman who won't take an opportunity when it's handed to her on a silver platter," he answered swiftly.

"You'd know all about silver platters! I didn't happen to be born with a silver spoon in my mouth, Mr. Spencer. I've had to *work* for what I've got. Yes, I've worked long and hard. You should try it sometime. It's good for the character," she sneered.

He clenched his jaw and gave the impression of counting to ten before replying. "A personal attack is the last resort when the *real* argument has been lost," he pointed out. *"Your* assessment of *my* character—a misguided assessment, I might add—is irrelevant."

"Not to me it isn't!" she said firmly. "I've put my whole life into this place. My life isn't for sale—not to you or anyone else."

"Making a job your whole life is another error," he answered simply.

How easy it was for him to say so. Olympian knowledge came easy from the lofty peaks he inhabited. What did *he* know about struggling, about unpaid bills and twelve-hour days and the indignity of begging for loans? What did he know about seeing his youth slipping away and never meeting any interesting people of the opposite sex? What did he know about the loneliness of only observing other people being happy? Without her awareness, Lisa's shoulders slumped, and her face mirrored these unhappy thoughts.

When she looked at David again, his hands made an involuntary motion toward her.

"Selling to you would be a worse error, and one I don't intend to make," she replied stiffly.

She watched as the sympathy faded from David's eyes and anger seeped in to replace it. But before he spoke, he had the anger under control, too. "Expansion isn't the answer," he said in a businesslike tone. "There *is* a demand for this kind of place, but it's a small, fairly local demand. You've caught your share of the market well enough. Honeymooners aren't going to come from out of state to stay here. It caters to folks who can't afford to travel far. You have nothing extraordinary to offer, except cheap prices. Too cheap, incidentally, which is your main problem. It's just a small, friendly little hotel—you can find one like it every fifty or so miles along the highways. You can't afford to develop the ski slope, and had no interest in the project in any case. Your best bet is to sell," he said and stood, waiting for her reaction.

"Best for *you*, you mean," she said, with a knowing expression.

"I'm not overlooking my own interests, certainly, but I'm thinking of you as well. Look, I know this weekend was a disaster. When I came, I planned to stay only one night and have a look around anonymously to see how things were going. I stayed because of *you*," he added, caressing her with those inky eyes.

She felt something within her go soft and was disgusted with herself. "I presume you didn't know at the time that your wife would be joining you?" she asked sharply.

"A wife seemed a likely companion for a weekend at a honeymoon hotel, so I invented one—my sister. I wanted a chance to observe your operation without arousing your suspicions to see how it's run. She arrived so late I had some hopes she wasn't coming at all, but once she was here, I knew she'd play the role to the hilt. Why else do you think I let you go so easily last night? It was only to spare you the melodramatics of her 'wifely' anger. Perhaps you've heard she's an actress," he added in explanation.

"I've also heard her name is Spencer, and that she has a daughter, which doesn't sound like an unmarried sister," Lisa pointed out. She feared after saying it that she might have stepped unwittingly on Marnie's toes. There were such things as single mothers nowadays, of course.

"She reverted to her maiden name when she got divorced. She has a daughter, so she still uses the title 'Mrs.' There's no big mystery in it. She's my sister. Marnie was always headstrong—a little spoiled," he added leniently. "She ran away and got married when she was eighteen. It lasted eleven months, till after Cathy was born. They live with Mom now. She was only playing a role this weekend —she's not really like that. I think you might even like her," he added uncertainly.

"I take the liberty of doubting that," Lisa said, but she admitted to a sense of relief at hearing it. The relief was short-lived. David was still trying to get her hotel away from her, and it was all she had. It had become her life. She lived, breathed, worked, and slept Paradise Inn. She'd be nothing without it. How could she just hand it over and take hard, cold cash in return? What would she *do* with herself? Then there was Leo to worry about, too.

"She's a bit hard on the nerves at times, I admit, but she's not a bad kid," David said defensively. "You can hardly deny she had some cause for complaint at least," he pointed out.

"Didn't we all?" she snipped. "You might as well go back to Mr. Pender. My answer is no, David. There are other banks besides yours. I'll get my loan, and I'll expand the inn. Maybe you'll drop in on us when you do get around to marrying someone," she suggested.

He crossed his arms and gazed at her, a long, enigmatic gaze. "After the other banks have turned you down, get back to me," he said in a quiet, commanding voice. "But don't wait too long. I want to get on with building this summer. Then, too, once you've gone bankrupt, your price will drop sharply. That's the way life is. I'll look forward to hearing from you, Lisa," he said with a long look.

"Don't hold your breath," she said, trying for an air of disinterest. While he still stood looking, she picked up a piece of paper from her desk and pretended she was reading it.

David didn't say good-bye. He just walked quietly out of her office and closed the door behind him. Through a blur of unshed tears, she noticed the paper in her fingers was a scrawled note from Lefty. The guests from room number six had stolen all the towels and face cloths when they left. A nice touch. Here she was, wearing herself ragged to provide a friendly, economical honeymoon haven for the less privileged classes, and they ripped her off in gratitude. No wonder she was going broke.

Leo, who was always sensitive to her needs, didn't come to her office. He knew she'd want to be alone a while to sort things out. The offer David made was tempting. It might be interesting to have a bank account in six black figures, instead of the five red ones she'd have if she expanded. Maybe she'd even start to think about selling, but she wouldn't sell to David Spencer, who only wanted to tear down the inn. Wouldn't she get a better price if she sold it all equipped to someone who wanted to run it as an inn? But soon she gave up any thought of selling. She'd go on with her plans of expansion, and raise her rates, too. They were the culprit—everything was going up, and her rates weren't keeping pace.

The phone rang, and she pulled herself back to the present. "Miss Burnes here," she said wearily.

"This is Lefty. How'd it go, Boss Lady? Did we get the money?"

"No, we didn't, Lefty."

"Tough beans, as we cucumbers say" was his message of condolence. Then he hung up and left her in dismal solitude.

She stayed in her office with the door closed while David checked out of the inn. He was the last person she wanted to see. It took some time to recoup her determination, to remind herself that no one could stop her from achieving her goal. Her goal was still a larger, improved inn. It had been for years, and she wouldn't let one troublesome customer with a whimsical sense of humor and disturbing eyes divert her.

Chapter Six

Lisa didn't waste a minute in applying elsewhere for a loan to expand her operation. The entire next week was spent in running from bank to bank with her briefcase of accounts and plans. The reply was inevitably the same. They were impressed with her industry and enthusiasm, but it was a borderline business—they didn't see the possibility for increased clients. One manager talked for half an hour about an advertising campaign she should undertake, but in the end he decided it would cost more than it would bring in in added revenues. Then, too, what she had to sell—well, it was interesting, but hardly of a sort to draw customers from afar. And her clientele was so limited, too, restricted to newlyweds. What were her views on changing it to a club for singles? Negative, she told him, and left. And when she got to the parking lot, her old van wouldn't start. It had to be towed to a garage and left overnight while she took an expensive cab home.

As June faded into July, Lisa conceded the banks were right. All those experts couldn't be wrong, so she decided she'd just continue along as she was, without the expansion. Why saddle herself with a huge debt that had to be paid off? But it was the death of a dream, and a person needs a dream to buoy up her unhappier hours.

There was another disappointment that she hadn't expected, in spite of the warnings. Lefty got his role as Mr. Cucumber in *Tossed Salad*. He disappeared one Monday morning without thinking to tell her till he was on his way out the door. He was gone only two days, but when he came back he wore a broad smile.

"Hi, Boss Lady. Hi and good-bye. I'm off to the bright lights of Off Broadway. You're looking at the new Mr. Cucumber," he told her. "I auditioned and got the job."

"Oh, Lefty, are you sure you want to be a cucumber?" Lisa asked, smiling wryly.

"It's not a bad thing to be," he told her with an air of self-importance. "Cucumbers are one of life's nourishers. Chock full of vitamins and all that good stuff. I have seventy-three lines," he added with satisfaction.

"That's wonderful. What does a cucumber say?" she asked, curious.

"Neat stuff. 'Get off my hill.' Cucumbers grow on hills. I didn't know that. And in the third act, I get a soliloquy, just before I'm picked to become a pickle. 'Oh, no, not the malt vinegar!' I say to Marnie. She's a carrot. Then at the end of the play, a guy comes along and takes a bite out of me, and I howl in pain and grief. It's not easy being a pickle, Boss. I've got to practice my howl. Something between a keening wail and a howl is what I'm after. Don't be worried if you hear me practicing."

"Don't practice too loud or you'll scare my customers," Lisa begged.

"Aggie, that's the present pregnant pickle, leaves next weekend. I'll practice here till then, and step in cold next Monday night. You'll be coming to see me sometime, of course," he told her, head wagging.

"I wouldn't miss it for the world. How much are tickets, and where do I get them?" Lisa asked, trying not to smile.

"For you, Boss Lady, they're gratis. I'll send you and Leo a pair after I'm broken in."

"That'll be nice."

"I don't plan to change, Boss. I'll still be the sweet old Lefty you always knew and loved, even when I'm a big star," he assured her.

"It'll be almost as good as being a pharaoh," she joked.

"Oh, Boss, don't tell me you believe in that reincarnation jazz!" he scoffed. "Marnie says it's a crock."

"How is Marnie?" she asked in a carefully casual tone.

"The kid's got talent. She's doing some commercials for TV. She is *so* clever, Boss. She went to an audition for a carrot juice commercial in her carrot outfit and got the job. Cute as a button in her green fern wig. And you'll see her next fall on a dustmop commercial, doing battle with dust balls. I wonder if they've cast the dustballs yet," he said to himself as he sauntered off, trying to look like a cucumber.

Lisa missed Lefty more than she thought she would. It was lonesome to pass the switchboard and not have him shout "Hi, Boss Lady." She had no one to tell her what life was. Life was an absent cucumber. She couldn't eat a tossed salad without thinking of Lefty, wondering.

But then her general mood was noticeably depressed. She felt as if she were waiting for something. Life seemed incomplete, as if it had been turned off at the most interesting part. She blamed it on the cancelled expansion project, but at the bottom of her heart she knew that was only a part of it. What she was really waiting for was to see that black head come through the door, smiling irreverently and joking about her corny place. Surely he'd call just once more to make sure she didn't want to sell her inn to him. One of these days he'd call, or come, and life would lose this uneasy, unfinished feeling.

And then there was the problem of Leo. He wouldn't admit for the world that he was old and tired, but in late July he came down with a bad cold and was off work. She had to nurse him, as well as fill his boots at the inn. She didn't realize till he was off duty how much he did for her. It seemed every time she turned around the cook was at her door with some minor problem. The chicken breasts didn't come, or the refrigerator had broken down and the meat had become tainted. The whipping cream was sour, too. Should he throw it out, or try to use it and hide the taste with more vanilla and sugar?

"Throw it out. We can't afford to risk food poisoning. Phone the dairy and ask them to send ice cream," she said, rubbing her brow.

"And what about the freezer? We can't use it as is. I've got ten pounds of frozen peas there on the verge of melting."

"Call the electrician, Herbert," she said patiently.

"He says it's not worth fixing. A new one of the size we need will cost over a thousand. I've got a line on a secondhand one from the dealer in town who took a trade-in, but he won't give us a warranty," the cook told her.

"How much does he want for it?"

"Four-fifty," he replied.

"Take it," Lisa said, feeling in her bones it was an unwise move, but a new one was out of the question. And Leo, poor Leo—his cough was getting worse.

On a Friday night she went to his room and found him feverish.

"I'm going to call the doctor, Leo," she said, worried.

"It's nothing a few days' rest won't cure," he assured her, but he'd already been in bed half a week.

Doc Abbott came to the inn and diagnosed pneumonia. How could Leo possibly have got pneumonia in the middle of summer? Lisa wondered. But at his age, the doctor pointed out, the lungs were weak and Leo admitted he'd been sleeping with his windows open and no blankets on. It was hot on the third floor, but sometimes by morning it had turned chilly. So they took Leo off to the hospital in Spelling.

After she finished worrying about Leo's health, she worried about paying the bill, on top of the new used freezer. It brought home to her in very graphic terms that David had been right. She was a borderline case. One more catastrophe and she was in debt. She'd have to get a mortgage, and how could she pay that off, when she was hardly making ends meet as it was? She realized, too, how much she'd depended on Leo's help.

Her life had become one long headache and worry. She almost dreaded opening her mail in the morning. If there was a cancellation in it, she'd cry. She needed every single customer she had booked. It was with trembling fingers that she tore open an envelope from New York. The Lattimers from New York had booked the Imperial Suite for the next week. He'd probably lost his job and they were cancelling the suite. The jolt her heart had initially given at sight of the New York postmark soon settled down. She knew instinctively David wouldn't send a cheap envelope with a smear in the corner. She smiled with relief and pleasure when she read the casual, familiar greeting:

Hi, Boss Lady,

Here are the tickets for the play that I promised you and Leo. Front row, center. Frankly, the play's a flop, between the green pepper that always forgets her lines, and the radish that remembers everybody's, and usually says them before we get a chance. Not to worry about old Lefty. Marnie's got me a job in two commercials. I get to wear a uniform in a muffler commercial—no speaking lines. My feet are going to be used in a corn-plaster commercial. Life's a mystery. You never know when your problems will become the solution. Hold that thought.

Sincerely,
Lefty

She looked at the date of the tickets he had sent. Friday—the first Friday in August. No hour was given, nor any address for the theater. She didn't see how she could possibly get away, yet something in her wanted very much to go. She was lonesome for Lefty, but she didn't forget that David lived in New York, too, and his sister was also in the play. Maybe he'd be there. . . .

She fell into a fit of musing as she gazed out with unseeing eyes at the ancient pine tree beyond her window. Why shouldn't she go to New York? Mrs. Latham could manage the place for one night. The world wouldn't stop turning if she took just one day away from the inn. She could leave at noon, have dinner and see the play, and drive back the same night. But then there was Leo. Such a lot of responsibilities weighed down on her drooping shoulders. She couldn't even get away for one evening. She began to feel a deep resentment toward the inn that had been her sole reason for living. Broken freezers and stolen towels and tainted cream occupied her thoughts. Where had the romance gone?

She reread Lefty's letter, but she didn't see how her problem inn could suddenly become her solution. That would only have been possible if she'd accepted David's offer to buy it. Was it too late? She reached for the New York phone book, at last accepting the possibility that she might sell. But David wanted to start building soon, and she had her reservations made months in advance, booked up till the end of August. She couldn't just cancel on all those young people who planned to honeymoon here. That wasn't fair.

That same afternoon, as she drove home from the hospital where she'd been visiting Leo, she stopped her car on the highway and looked all up and down the mountain. There was no sign of building or ski trails being cut. Maybe David hadn't started work yet, then. Lisa felt a little ray of hope, till she rethought that tumultuous conversation in her office the day David left. He'd mentioned building on the other side of the mountain if he couldn't buy her place.

She continued her drive till she reached the other side, and there she saw it. A new gravel road had been put in, leading to a valley nestled in the hills. Wilmar Construction had a sign up announcing the site of the new ski lodge. So it was all settled, and she, so busy these days, hadn't even heard about it. Now that it was too late, she knew she should have accepted David's offer.

She was curious to see how the place was progressing. A glance at her watch showed it was after five. The construction people would be gone by now, so she figured it would be a good time to drive in and take a peek. Then again, if her van decided to break down again, she'd be stranded alone in the hills, with night coming on.

The woodcutters had been working on the southern slope of Cobbler's Mountain, clearing stands of trees to make the ski runs. The raw paths twisted through the greenery like giant snakes. Strange metal shafts had begun to rise out of the mountainside that Lisa assumed would eventually become ski lifts.

She got out of her van and walked around the empty building site. A large area had been cleared and staked out with pegs. If this was to be the lodge, it was enormous. It looked as though excavation was about to begin. Yellow tractors with scoops stood ready for the job. Already the construction company had a temporary prefab hut set up. Looking all around, she saw a yellow truck parked by the side of the hut. It had the Wilmar Construction sign on the side of the door.

Lisa was suddenly aware that she was trespassing and turned to go back to her van, in case the driver of that truck was still in the hut. As she opened the car door, a man came out of the building, looking behind him. He wore work clothes and brown boots. She waited a moment to explain her presence, thinking it would look suspicious if she just drove off without speaking.

While she waited, another man walked out behind the first. She didn't notice that he, too, wore work clothes and boots. She noticed only his black head, glinting in the sun as he lowered it to get through the doorway. David's head had looked the very same the first time she saw him. He looked up and saw her, and the same startled expression settled on his features as had done in Ophelia's Garden. Lisa had a flashing sense of *déjà vu* and wished she could turn back the clock and begin the last months of her life over again. As she stood staring, he took a step toward her.

Chapter Seven

As David came toward her, she noticed he was wearing jeans and a blue and white cotton shirt that jarred with her earlier memories of him, in which he was always sleek and debonair. His face was darker too, now weathered to walnut from exposure to the sun.

"Lisa, what are you doing here?" he asked, staring at her. "Is something the matter?" His voice held a note of alarm.

She knew her shock must be mirrored in her face. "No, I was passing by and drove down to see how the ski lodge is coming along," she answered. "I hope you don't mind."

"No, of course not," he said, but he looked as ill at ease as she felt. "I was just surprised to see you. Let me show you around," he offered with a little tentative smile.

He turned aside and spoke to the man with him. The man got into the truck and left, revealing David's Lotus parked behind it.

"I was going to call you this evening," he said. "It must be ESP or something. Lefty could tell us all about it. I came over this morning to check out the ski trails and meet with the Wilmar people. How's everything going at your hotel?" he asked in a friendly way, quite at ease now.

"Not too bad," she parried, unwilling to admit the state of chaos she'd sunk into.

"I figured you'd managed to pull things together since you never called me. I assume you've raised your rates," he stated, so she didn't feel she had to answer. "Did you get your loan?" he asked, with no ill will as far as she could tell.

"No, I'm just carrying on as things were," Lisa answered briefly, looking around at the site, and tacitly inviting him to begin his tour.

"I'm glad to hear you took my advice. The hotel's intimacy was one of its chief assets." He followed her gaze, and when she didn't answer, he began the tour. "There's not much to show you here yet. You can tell by the markers where the excavation for the main lodge will begin next week. This is the ski store and rental shop over here," he said, walking off to the right, where a smaller area was marked off.

She followed him, looking at the markers, but in her mind's eye she saw only David. "I hope our construction won't interfere with your operation, but with the mountain between us, I don't think you'll get much noise or dust," he said, striking a cheerful, reassuring tone.

There seemed more than a physical mountain between them. He was treating her like any chance guest, when her heart was fluttering in excitement to be with him again. She schooled her tone to his and replied, "I'm sure I won't. I didn't even realize work had begun here till I happened to see the new road from the highway and decided to drive down for a look.''

"We get a lot of local visitors," he said blandly. "I guess everyone's interested."

"How many trails do you plan to clear?" she questioned, deciding that since she was being treated as a tourist, she might as well behave like one.

"Fortunately for us there were a few natural trails that didn't require more than a dozen trees being taken down to clear them completely. The broad, shallow clearing there is for beginners," he said, pointing up the hill. "We'll have a couple of instructors on hand for the novices. The steep, curving path that goes up to the top is the more challenging hill, for experts only, and there are a couple of intermediate trails."

She followed his pointing hand with her eyes, and when she'd seen all the hills, she glanced at David. His clean, strong profile stood out against the green curve of hills in the distance. He looked remote as an eagle, though he stood only a yard from her. Then he suddenly turned toward her, and she saw that there was no suggestion of remoteness in his eyes as he peered down at her. "Do you ski at all?" he asked.

"I used to a little when I was young," she said.

"Now that you're old and arthritic, you've given it up?" he teased with a charming smile. A warm rush of emotion swept through her as he placed his hand on her elbow and turned away from the mountain to walk her back to her van.

"I don't seem to have time for it," she said dismissively.

"Surely winter is your off season!" he objected.

"Yes, but there were no ski runs close by before. Perhaps

I'll tackle it this winter," she said, looking back to the beginners' slope. That didn't look too treacherous, she thought.

"I hope so. I plan to spend a lot of time here. New York isn't that far away, and I don't have to be there for business every day." Did she imagine the mute suggestion in those dark eyes, the hint that maybe they'd spend some of that time together? After a pause, he continued. "Actually this is my major project at the moment. I was lucky to find a relatively treeless mountain that offered a good variety of runs so close to home, since I love to ski."

They reached the van, but Lisa was loath to climb into it and leave. David didn't reach to open the door either, but stood waiting, watching. After a moment he said, "It's pretty over this way." He led her off to the right of the area cleared for building. She was happy that David, too, seemed to want to prolong their meeting.

They strolled together toward the foot of Cobbler's Mountain. A few yards beyond the construction site, the natural vegetation was undisturbed. Tall grass brushed their legs and entangled their feet, making progress slow. She noticed that already the early flowers of summer had gone. There were no dandelions, no violets, no daisies, but a random scattering of wild asters and mustard. She remembered her mother telling her when the wildflowers changed from white to purple and gold, the summer was waning. Where had it gone? She couldn't remember seeing even one daisy the past two months. She hadn't taken a moment to look for them. Had there been lilies of the valley and violets this summer?

A sweet warbling filled the air, and she stopped to scan the nearby trees. A bright flash of red swooped down to the ground. "Oh, look, a cardinal!" she exclaimed, smiling.

"I've seen a lot of them around here," David said, stopping beside her. "His mate should be along soon. They're very chummy, the cardinals. You usually see them together, like inhabitants of Paradise Inn," he said on a teasing note.

As they stood still, watching, the female flew down and joined her mate. She was less flashy, a brownish bird with some red markings. "Her feathers aren't quite so fine as hubby's, but that's Mrs. Cardinal, all right. See her crest?" David said, watching them with interest till they flew away.

"I wouldn't have taken you for a bird lover. Where'd you learn about birds, living in New York?" Lisa asked, using it as an excuse to gaze at him, to store up an image of his face for later when she was alone.

"My folks had a bungalow in the country. Besides, doesn't everyone indulge in some tender nonsense where birds are concerned? We're jealous of their freedom. That's what it is," he said lightly, but there was a wistful smile as he searched the trees for the cardinals.

They walked to the edge of the treeline. "It'll be cooler in here," David said, and he began to weave his way through the trees.

"I should be getting back," Lisa told him without much conviction. It was pleasant walking, with the slippery surface of fallen pine needles underfoot and the trees tall as cathedrals all around. Patches of light shimmered above the interlocking branches. The pungent smell of pine gum oozing from the trees unlocked childhood memories of summers spent roaming these minor forests. A bank of ferns appeared as if by magic, swaying enticingly in the shade of the trees. Ferns liked shade and moisture, Lisa mused. There might even be a brook nearby.

"So should I," David admitted, "but I consider it a duty

to squeeze a few minutes of pleasure out of every day. I don't suppose the real Garden of Eden was anything like this, but I always think of it in these isolated, unspoiled pockets of nature,'' he said musingly, stopping to look all around.

"It's beautiful," Lisa said softly, feeling a nostalgia for lost youth. The land around her own inn was similar to this, but she'd hardly set foot in the forest the past two years. What enchantment she'd been robbing herself of.

She glanced up to see David staring at her. The sun dappled his face with moving spots of light and shade; they danced on his shoulders in changing patterns as the branches swayed overhead. Behind him, the tall trees rose in stately columns, their magnificence given a homey touch by the scampering of a chipmunk along a low branch.

"Thank you for showing me this," she said simply. "It's so . . . idyllic."

"It's the way the world should be," he replied, still gazing at her, with a new intentness stealing into his eyes. "Lisa." The word was quiet as a sigh. His arms went around her waist, drawing her against him, while his head came down to hers, slowly, irrevocably, ending in a kiss.

The warmth from his body seeped through the thin summer covering of shirts to make her acutely aware of his physical presence. His chest was a solid, human substance anchoring her to the here-and-now, while his lips wafted her off to another land. She heard the faint rustling from the branches. Then his lips moved on hers, and she heard only the blood throbbing in her veins, answering the primeval call of nature. His moist tongue moved seductively against her lips, coercing her will to his. Her lips parted and he gently possessed her mouth.

The warm pressure of his fingers stroking her back slid

lower, while pulling her inexorably closer, till she felt one with him. A tumultuous emotion in her breast moved her to his rhythm as he shifted against her, fitting her to the firm contours of his body. One hand moved, cupped her head, his fingers massaging her scalp, while his lips pressed harder, insistently. The gentle tongue became demanding, and her blood answered the call. There was an aching need in her for this moment, this sharing with another human being. The long, hard years had passed, and she hadn't squeezed her share of pleasure from them. It was so pleasant here with David—his Adam to her Eve.

His head lifted, and his dark eyes scrutinized her with unblinking intensity, as though looking into her very soul. He swallowed once, then took her hand and they walked on without saying a word. The babbling of a stream lured them on, past the ferns to a moss-cushioned bank. They sat down, and Lisa kicked off her sandals to dabble her feet in the cool, running water. David unbuttoned his shirt and flapped the tails to trap the cool breezes. He reached for her hands and, with a questioning look, as though seeking permission, pulled them under his shirt against his warm flesh. She wrapped her arms around him, her cheek resting against his chest. The pleasant male aroma of perspiration and soap stirred her senses, joined with the crisp brush of his chest hair to excite her.

David leaned above her, lowering her till she was reclining against the ground with his head and shoulders looming above her. His lips just brushed hers, thrilling her with the promise of a kiss rather than kissing her. He unbuttoned her shirt and trailed his fingers lightly over the swell of velvet breasts, while a shivering excite through her body. She felt his lips neck, and a gurgle of ti sounded strange, almost foreign to her own ears. How long was it since she'd laughed out loud? Too long! Life was escaping her, but it was here in her arms now, free for the taking.

She turned her head aside and eagerly opened her lips to his when they sought hers. Her head was pushed against the mossy bank, while his kiss seared her, pulled her passion along to soar into the wavering branches above. His moving fingers tantalized her breasts, then traced patterns downward, rough against her sensitive skin, and encircled her waist, squeezing gently while her bones turned to water. She ran her fingers up his back in feathery motions, over the bulge of tensed muscles, up to his shoulders, caressing their contours with sensuous strokes, sweeping into the narrower column of his proud neck, bent in submission now above her. An encouraging croon rumbled deep in his throat as the tips of her fingers caressed him, roaming up to the base of his skull with swirling, luxurious motions.

It was a perfect setting for love, in this cool, shadowy glade, with the sun dropping now, a copper ball with a halo of golden slivers shimmering through the treetops. David's head nestled in the hollow of her neck. His tongue flicked against her ear, a teasing, playful motion. He lifted his head and smiled at her, his face so close it was blurred. Or was it her lowered lashes that caused those iridescent prisms to flicker?

"I'm in no condition to be so close to you. I've been climbing mountains, and I'm filthy," he said. "I'm staying overnight in Spelling. Why don't I go there and shower? We'll go out tonight and paint the town red!" he said with a smile.

She felt a brief instant's joy before reality settled on her like a blanket. How could she possibly get away, with

Leo in the hospital, and no one to handle the evening's entertainment at the inn? A hot ball of resentment burned in her chest. The inn had become a tyrant, worse than a boss. It had taken over her life. She didn't even have time for love. When she spoke, her voice was tinged with bitterness.

"I'm afraid it's impossible, David."

His face stiffened, first into curiosity, then latent offense. She rushed on to overcome it. "The thing is, Leo is not at all well. I'm handling things pretty well on my own for a while."

The spell was broken. They sat up, adjusting their clothing about them. "I'm sorry to hear about Leo. What's the matter with him?" he asked, but in a cool voice.

"Pneumonia. Don't ask how he got it in July, but he got it. He's in the hospital, actually. And with Lefty gone, too . . ." Her voice trailed off into silence, while a sad sense of imprisonment overcame her. David arose and pulled her up from the mossy bank.

"Perhaps later in the evening, after dinner . . ." was David's next suggestion.

There was a wiener roast planned for that evening out by the pool. Someone had to supervise it, and that wasn't the end of her duties either. Someone had to check out the reservations and tend to the hundred and one things that had to be handled: making up bills, going over the kitchen details with the cook, chasing the maids to make sure they'd done their jobs. She now spent the entire evening between the office and the dance hall or other supervised activity. She wasn't eager to hire an expensive assistant either. She was a virtual prisoner, but she didn't intend to whine and complain to David Spencer, who had offered her a way out.

"I'll be pretty busy all evening," she said calmly, as though it didn't matter much.

He gave her a sharp, examining look. "I hope you're not trying to run the entire operation yourself, Lisa. Have you hired staff to replace Lefty and Leo?" he asked.

"Leo won't be gone long. Of course I haven't replaced him."

"Couldn't I see you, just for an hour?" he persisted. "I'll drive out to the inn." There was an intent eagerness in his eyes.

But she couldn't spare even an hour. "Not this time," she said, then walked back through the trees, with a silence heavy on the air. He was hurt—naturally he couldn't understand her life. How could he? No one would believe she was such a fool. She tried to think of some neutral subject to end the meeting on a pleasant note.

"Have you seen *Tossed Salad?*" she asked in a conversational way.

"Several times. I consider it a family duty to support my sister," he answered in the same spirit. "Have you seen it?"

"Not yet. Lefty sent me tickets," she mentioned.

"Do you plan to use them?" he asked at once, with sharp interest.

"Possibly. I'm due for a weekend in New York. How is Lefty, anyway, in his role of Mr. Cucumber, I mean?" she asked.

"What can I say?" he asked, throwing out his hands. "As cucumbers go, I guess he's all right. As far as I know, there's nothing to compare it to. I don't believe Olivier or Gielgud or any of those gents have ever tackled a similar role. But it's amusing," he finished. "I think you'd enjoy it. At least my fear that Marnie would end up marrying the pharaoh has left me. It's petered out into friendship."

"Lefty mentioned she helped him get some commercial

work in TV," she said, trying to keep the conversation going so she wouldn't have to leave.

"I think you'd enjoy the play. Be sure to give me a call if you decide to take him up on the offer. Here, I'll give you my card," he said, rifling in his pockets for one.

She took it and put it carefully in her wallet. "Thanks for the tour," she said, taking a last look around at the ski slopes and the construction site.

David seemed equally reluctant to let her go. He looked at his watch, then at Lisa. "It's early yet. Why don't we go somewhere and have a nice, cold drink? You won't be serving dinner for a while yet." He waited with a sense of held breath in the air between them.

When she didn't reply, he said softly, encouragingly, "We have a lot to talk about."

Every fiber of her being wanted to go, but she thought of that uncertain freezer back at the inn. If there was a crisis in the kitchen . . . She'd told them she'd be back in an hour when she went to the hospital, and she'd already been gone more than twice that long. She had to arrange the shifts for tomorrow, too. No, it was out of the question.

"Give me a rain check," she said, softening her refusal with a smile.

"No, *you* give *me* a chance," he countered. "I know you must have singularly unpleasant memories of that disastrous weekend at your inn. I've regretted the mess I made of it a dozen times."

"No, really! You don't have to apologize, David," she assured him.

"I was wrong about your making a go of it, so I *do* have to apologize," he insisted. "And I want to compliment you on your ingenuity, too. I admire your skill."

She felt a compelling desire to correct this erroneous

impression. She wanted to throw herself on his chest and admit he had been right; it was too much. She was weary with work and worry. "Thanks, we all make mistakes," she said.

"*I* certainly did, but I'm not about to make another. Lisa, I want to see you before I go back to New York. *You* set the time. Nobody works twenty-four hours a day." She saw the determined set of his jaw and knew he wasn't going to be put off easily.

But what was the point in prolonging the pain? In the end he'd always be going back to New York, to his life that was light-years removed from hers. He'd be going to parties and shows while she continued her unending work. It wasn't *fair!* But she couldn't tell him the truth about her life. She didn't want his pity; she preferred his admiration.

"Oh, what's the point?" she exclaimed, frustration lending an angry tinge to her words.

"What's *usually* the point of a man wanting to see a woman?" he answered. His fingers bit into the muscles of her upper arms. He didn't quite shake her, but she knew he wanted to. His brows were drawn together in a scowl.

"I guess that depends on the man—and the woman," she answered nonchalantly. She was triumphant at having disturbed him, at having that much power over his emotions.

"What am I supposed to conclude from that speech?" he asked sharply. His hands released her arms and fell to his sides. "Not ten minutes ago you wanted me. Don't deny it." His scowl assumed a puzzled look.

"I want lots of things. You're not at the top of my list. Sorry, David. I really have to go now."

"Who's at the top?" he asked, his eyes narrowing.

"Not who—*what!* How do you think I saved my inn? By

constant devotion," she said. There was a new air of playfulness in her answer. It did her a world of good to know she held some power over David's feelings. She could rouse him to anger and frustration, even if only for a few moments.

"I refuse to be jealous of an inn!" he said, somewhat mollified.

"The timing is just wrong, David, with Leo sick and everything. Try me next time you're in town."

"You can depend on it. And you can warn that inn it has some competition. I'll call you next time."

"Good. Thanks again for the tour. Bye." She turned and got into her van, started the engine, and lifted her hand to wave good-bye.

He didn't move from the spot, but before she pulled away, he called, "Don't forget to phone me if you come to New York."

"For sure," she called, then drove off with a scrunch of gravel and a cloud of dust that robbed her of a last look at him. Back to Paradise Inn, which was fast becoming her private hell. The sink in the Blue Room had gotten clogged and overflowed, wetting the carpet. Careless patrons, Lisa thought angrily—what had they dropped down it and not told anyone? The plumber couldn't come for two days. She'd have to shift the McCormacks out of the Blue Room to clog up another drain.

At least the freezer was holding up. The whipped cream in the dessert was fine, but if she had to eat another plate of sponge cake and fruit and whipped cream, she'd gag.

Mrs. Latham went to the hospital that evening to see Leo and dropped in on her way home to report. She thought he looked pale and thin, but he was coughing less and insisted he felt much better. Maybe it was the bottle of Scotch that

Mr. Spencer fellow had brought him that accounted for it. In any case, Doc Abbott didn't want him going back to work too soon. A month at least to recuperate, he suggested.

Lisa took note of this, and of the fact that David had visited him. That was thoughtful of him. She went to the pool to see that everything was ready for the wiener roast. The girl now in charge of the pool had put in too much chlorine. It reeked to high heaven, and God only knew what it might do to the eyes of the customers. She warned them to be careful and was happy to see most of them wearing the masks provided for water games. Much as Lisa complained about Lefty, he had always kept the pool in perfect condition. He liked being at the pool in his white shorts to receive the girls' admiration, but he did a lot of vacuuming and cleaning up while he was there.

She'd looked forward to having that pool installed with so much pleasure, but she hadn't been in it more than three times the whole month. Was she crazy, or just too stubborn to behave rationally? Why did she do it? Why was she here running a wiener roast, when she could be out with David Spencer? There had to be more to life than working and worrying.

She *would* go to New York in August. She'd call David and have a wonderful time. She didn't care if every customer in the hotel left without paying his bill; she'd go. She needed at least one day away from all this. Self-exploiting. That's what her operation was. David had hit it on the head. She was killing herself to provide a bargain holiday for strangers—strangers who clogged her drains and stole her towels.

*   *   *

Leo came home from the hospital the next Monday, and though she wouldn't let him work, he was there, on the premises in his room to make a decision if any calamity should occur.

"I'm worried about you," she said, tucking him into bed on the afternoon he arrived.

"I'm a tough old rooster. I'll be all right. To tell the truth, Lisa, it's *you* I'm worried about," he said, examining her. "You're pale and thin. Why don't you go out to that nice pool and sunbathe? Take a dip, get yourself some tan," he urged.

"I don't tan anyway. I'll just get freckled," she said.

"There's nothing wrong with a sprinkling of freckles. Don't worry about me. I've got my medicine right here, and the girls will be popping in from time to time to check up on me. Run along now. I'm going to have a nap," Leo said. And he looked as if he needed one.

"I've been thinking of a different holiday for myself," she said. "I'd like to go to New York and see Lefty's play. I wish you could come with me. He sent two tickets," she reminded him.

"Give young Spencer a call. His sister's in it, too, as I recall. He seems a nice lad. Mighty fine Scotch he brought to the hospital for me." He smiled in memory.

"That was sweet of him," she said. "Yes, I'll give him a call. He asked me to, in fact," she said, with a thought of his card in her wallet.

"There you are, then. He'll be a more amusing date than this old carcass. I'm delighted to hear you're going."

"I'll go only if you're completely well, so get busy and get better," she ordered playfully.

"Is everything going all right with the business, Lisa?"

Leo asked with a worried frown. "You haven't been keeping anything from me, just because I'm ill?"

"Everything's fine. Just the usual annoyances. The situation's desperate, but not serious, as usual," she told him.

Things were a little better with Leo back. Even if he couldn't work, he was there to talk to and discuss matters with. By Friday, the day before her projected visit to New York, Leo was no longer spending the whole day in bed. He had been downstairs a few times and seemed well on the road to recovery.

"The only thing I don't like about this trip is your notion of coming back alone at night," Leo told her. "It's madness, Lisa. Stay over for the night and come back in the morning. You'd be here by noon."

"You're right. I don't know what I was thinking of. I'd have to go to bed and sleep till noon if I came back the same night anyway, so I'll sleep over," she decided.

"You'd better make a reservation," he told her.

"I'll call Lefty and ask him to do it for me. The hotels may be busy and it could take a few calls."

"That's a good idea," Leo agreed and watched as she placed the call.

"No trouble, Boss Lady. Will do. You can count on old Lefty," Lefty assured her.

The morning of her departure was a busy one. Lisa selected and packed her clothes and chose accessories—all squeezed in between her regular inn duties. She carefully packed her favorite dress—a pale green halter-style sundress that plunged daringly in front and flared out in a wide circle below. A short hand-crocheted jacket was included in case, by some miracle, the weather turned chilly. In her mind, she floated on a dance floor beneath the stars with David somewhere in New York for half of that morning. She didn't suppose there was an open-air dance place in New York, but fantasies didn't have to worry about mundane facts like that. It was going to be a wonderful holiday. She felt in her bones that when she came back everything would have changed. Things would be settled between her and David. She'd no longer be a prisoner to others, but free to live her own life.

Chapter Eight

Lisa felt like a truant when she struck out for New York, leaving her worries behind her. She stayed at the inn till luncheon had been served. Every detail of the next twenty-four hours was carefully arranged for her staff: menus, activities, shifts, arrivals, and departures. Nothing could go wrong. No, nothing *should* go wrong, she revised, crossing her fingers on the steering wheel.

The day was gorgeous, bright and sunny, but with a cooling breeze that prevented the van from becoming an oven. The scenery as she drove through the Poconos was lovely, with green hills rising all around her. Sumacs sat like opened umbrellas in spots, with taller, more majestic fir trees soaring in the distance. Though the traffic was heavy with tourists, there were no disastrous delays due to construction or accidents. Lisa was a little nervous driving into New York at the evening traffic hour, but Lefty had given her good instructions. He was meeting her at the theater, and with the address memorized, she didn't see how she could go wrong.

Lefty stood at the curb waiting for her. He sauntered forward, with a pale green sport shirt hanging loose over fawn trousers. He'd let his hair grow longer, and with its tendency to wave, it looked rather unkempt. She remembered Leo's old battle with him to keep it cut short to present a neat appearance. Lefty didn't look particularly neat, but perhaps he'd turned Bohemian to honor his new job.

"Welcome to the Big Apple, Boss Lady," he said. "You can stash your wheels behind the theater. I arranged it." He climbed into the front seat with her and pointed to an alleyway ahead. "We'll go into the dressing room for a drink and discuss plans," he added, so much like himself that she wanted to hug him.

She locked her van and Lefty led her through a low door into a dismal, dark hallway, till they came to a barn of a room with several cheap mirrors on the wall, and a rack of strange costumes hanging on a wheeled storage dolly.

"This is my spot," he said proudly, straddling a chair in front of one of the mirrors. Each actor had a shelf under the mirror to hold his makeup and personal paraphernalia. "Grab yourself a chair and we'll talk," he invited.

She pulled the chair from the next mirror up to his and sat down with a sigh.

"Want a drink?" he asked, looking her over closely.

"I'd love one. I'm baked," she answered, envisioning a cold glass of something.

"Whatever Lisa wants, Lisa gets," he said grandly. He pulled a bottle of cheap red wine up from the floor. There were two paper cups on his shelf. He unscrewed the wine cap and poured them both a shot of the warm wine. "Here's to old times," he said, touching her paper cup with his. Then he drank. "How's Leo? All back in shape?" he asked.

"He's coming along. It's nice to see you again, Lefty. We all missed you."

"Mutual, Boss. Give them all my regards," he said, taking another sip.

"What hotel did you get for me, Lefty? I'd like to go and shower and change. It was so hot and dusty in the van."

"No room at the inns. Sorry, full up. You can bunk on my sofa," he told her calmly.

"You mean you didn't get me a hotel room! Oh, Lefty!" she exclaimed, visions of her cooling shower vanishing.

"You didn't want to drop one-fifty for a night's sleep, did you?" Lefty asked, shaking his head in the old way that was beginning to annoy her again already.

"There must have been something cheaper than that!" she countered.

"Even that was as scarce as a turtle's teeth. No problem. I have lots of room. We'll grab a bite before the play. There's a drugstore down a few blocks that has edible chili," he mentioned. A hot, spicy dish of any sort didn't sound edible in this weather, but Lisa assumed there'd be more than chili on the menu.

"I wanted to freshen up and change," she told him, looking at her denim skirt and cotton shirt. "I don't want to go to the theater like this." She especially didn't want to meet David afterward without changing.

"Not to worry. You look fine. This isn't Broadway, Boss. Most of the audience wears jeans. Last night they both wore shorts it was so hot."

"*Both?*" she asked, staring.

"It was a slow night. Sometimes we get twenty or thirty.

Our capacity's a hundred. Want to see the stage?" he offered, with no embarrassment at these revelations.

"Sure," she agreed, setting down the cup of warm wine, glad to be rid of it.

They passed a soft-drink machine in the hallway, and she got a soda. The stage was a dusty little square of weathered wood with a proscenium arch giving a view of a few rows of folding chairs placed more or less at random.

"The roar of the greasepaint, the smell of the crowd," Lefty said in a bored voice and looked at her to see her reaction.

She viewed the depressing sight for a moment, with her heart sinking. "I'd be glad to have you back at Paradise Inn, Lefty, if this isn't working out," she said, feeling sorry for him.

"Give up show biz?" he asked, astonished. "Hey, them's fighting words. You'll feel the magic tonight."

He turned around and strolled back to his changing room, and she followed him. "It was just an idea," she said, peering into the dark corners, where a scuttling sound suggested the presence of rodents.

"That's okay. After we fold, I might take you up on the offer. The muffler commercial didn't work out. In the other one, they're using just my feet. That's cheaper for them. Do you want to eat now?"

"I'd like to make a phone call first. David Spencer asked me to call him. We . . . uh . . . might be going out later, actually," she added, hoping Lefty wouldn't be hurt. But he certainly hadn't gone out of his way to welcome or entertain her. "We might go out for dinner."

"That's cool, Boss Lady. I'll meet the rest of the cast at the drugstore. It's a tradition. There's the ding-a-ling," he said, nodding to a pay phone on the far wall.

"Thanks."

She got out her card and called David's number, with an excitement churning in her breast. The phone rang two or three times, and she let it go on ringing. She looked at the card, noticing it was his business card he had given her. Glancing at her watch, she saw it was a quarter to six. He must have left his office. She hung up and reached for the phone book.

She looked through the rows of Spencers for a David or D. There were nine of the latter and two Davids. "You wouldn't happen to know where he lives, I suppose?" she asked Lefty.

"Town house on Sixty-second Street. Probably an unlisted number," he said with very little interest.

"Oh." She looked again and saw none of the Spencers with a D. lived on Sixty-second Street.

"You can get his number from Marnie tonight," he suggested. "And don't forget your money in the Return slot." She fished it out.

"I'd like to get the number from Marnie now. Would you mind phoning her for me?" she asked, reluctant to call that troublesome woman.

"She's not home. She's taking her kid to some birthday party this afternoon. She'll be here by seven-thirty. Let's eat."

Lisa turned to him, shoulders sagging, lips turned down in disappointment. For this she had driven all afternoon, run off from her tottering business—to eat chili in a drugstore with a bunch of hapless hippies. She couldn't even change into clean clothes, and she didn't intend to spend the night on Lefty's lumpy sofa either.

"Sure, let's eat," she said, resigned.

The drugstore restaurant had a choice of chili or tacos.

She figured the chili would be harder to make inedible, and chose it. It didn't taste quite as bad as it looked. It couldn't—it looked like watered-down dog food. She met the radishes and tomatoes and beans that made up the cast of *Tossed Salad*. They weren't bad people really, but she had nothing in common with them. Their talk was all show talk, all of it as unrealistic and optimistic as Lefty's had originally been. In this group, Lefty seemed relatively normal. She listened forlornly and ate a little of the hot chili and wondered where David was.

At seven-thirty on the dot, Marnie Spencer came in. She was so startlingly different from the rest of the cast it was hard to believe she was one of them. She wore an extremely fashionable white cotton dress that set off her tan and trim figure to advantage. Her hair was a golden halo, her makeup well applied, but she sat down and joined in their talk with apparent relish.

"You remember Lisa Burnes," Lefty reminded Marnie.

"Of course, from that quaint little inn in the Poconos. How is it? Still out of towels?" Marnie asked with a gay laugh, all bitterness forgotten. It had been a game for her that weekend.

"She wants David's phone number," Lefty said, always blunt.

"What on earth for?" Marnie asked, curiosity shining in her blue eyes. "David's already chosen another spot for the ski lodge, if that's what you're calling him for."

"No, he asked me to call him when I was in New York," Lisa said, feeling forward.

"He's not home. David's out with his girl friend," Marnie said, with no particular emphasis or malice as far as Lisa could judge. She was just stating a simple fact. That it happened to be devastating to her listener wasn't even noticed. Marnie gave her the number, but there was obviously no point in using it now.

"I suppose you've seen David, now that he spends some time at the construction site?" Marnie asked.

"Yes, I talked to him last week," Lisa said, adding no details.

"And how is the lodge coming along?" Marnie asked.

"It's coming along nicely," Lisa told her. That was about all they had to say to each other.

The party soon left to walk the two blocks back to the theater. There was a hand-painted sign out front advertising the show. The theater was called The Summer Show House. Lisa was surprised to see snippets of reviews from respectable drama critics quoted in the advertisements. The words "hilarious," "interesting," "novel," and "ingenious" were enlarged, giving some hope for the evening's entertainment. She phoned David's home on the chance that his date had been cancelled, but he wasn't there. The answering machine asked for a message, and she said only that Lisa Burnes had called and was sorry to miss him. He knew where she'd be, if he arrived in time to join her, so she didn't have to tell him. She hadn't much hope of seeing him.

She gave her ticket at the door and went to sit all alone in the dark theater while the cast prepared for the performance. A few people straggled in, about fifteen in all. Every time the sound of footsteps was heard, she looked eagerly around hoping it might by some miracle be David. But of course if he came, he'd probably be with his date. Foolish of her not to have notified him in advance. Why had she thought he'd be sitting home alone every night, an attractive and desirable man like David Spencer? Why had she thought that, because he asked her out for a drink a week ago, he was sitting waiting by the phone for her call? He was just being polite; he probably felt sorry for her if the truth were known.

It was a very odd play. There were some hilarious moments, but they were mostly accidental. She didn't think the "cucumber" was supposed to fall off his hill and emit a quite audible curse at the radish. There was some underlying message in the play suggesting that man and nature cooperate to survive on this planet, but it was hazy— perhaps a poor translation from the French. It was certainly novel and ingenious, as advertised, but it didn't appear likely it would be beckoned to move to Broadway. It would die a quick death, unless the producers decided to perform euthanasia and close it.

Lisa clapped very hard when it was over to make up for the people who had left halfway through it, and the desultory applause of the half dozen who sat through till the end. The whole atmosphere was so informal that when the curtain closed, Lisa just climbed up on the stage and went through the curtain to join Lefty in the changing room, leaving time for the men to get into their trousers.

She was leaning against the wall in the hallway having another soda when the ladies' changing room door opened and Marnie Spencer came out. "Oh, hi, Lisa. Are you coming with Lefty and me?" she asked with a friendly smile.

"I was supposed to meet him after the play," she replied, learning for the first time that she would be crashing in on Marnie's date.

"That's nice. We'll all have a drink somewhere before taking you to your hotel," Marnie said, making it clear who was in charge of the evening. Wait till she found out there was no hotel room! David thought there was only friendship between his sister and Lefty, but it seemed a very close friendship indeed.

Marnie walked forward and entered the men's dressing room, which occasioned no shrieks, despite the semi-dressed bodies Lisa glimpsed through the opened door. Marnie Spencer was a free spirit—she did what she wanted to, without much thought to the consequences. David must be at his wits' end with her.

David . . . He was seldom out of her thoughts. No sign of him. She looked up and down the dark corridor, but the only sounds were the babbling from the dressing rooms and a buzz as a fly flew past her face.

Before long, Marnie and Lefty emerged from the men's dressing room, looking a very incongruous pair. She noticed Lefty still had traces of green makeup behind his ears.

"Now for a little jubilation," Lefty declared, and they all went out into the street, where the muggy air engulfed them. Lisa wondered if Lefty would be allowed into a nice night spot in his loose sport shirt without a tie, but she needn't have worried. The spot they went to could hardly be called decent, let alone nice. It was a dingy little bar so dark no one could possibly see what he was wearing.

"Set 'em up, Joe. The usual," Lefty said. "The usual, all around."

They each got a glass of beer, and Lefty snatched a wooden bowl of pretzels from the counter. He ate every one of them while they talked. Marnie talked mostly about various assignments her agent was working on. As she had an independent income, she worked mainly for the satisfaction it brought, and the interesting people she met.

"If you sign with my agent, Lefty, he could do wonders for your career as well," she mentioned more than once.

"I'm thinking of heading out to L.A. when the show folds," Lefty told her. "Go west, young man. The land of milk and honey. Never rains in sunny California. A guy could probably live on the beach."

This unlikely domicile was discussed a while, but Lisa only half listened. Oh, why had she come here? It was possibly the worst evening of her life. And while they were here, there was no possibility of David's finding them. But then that possibility had pretty well dwindled to zero in any case. She hardly wanted to be found in her dusty travel clothes.

"All set, kids?" Lefty asked after they had each had a second glass of beer.

"Can I drop you somewhere, Lisa?" Marnie asked. She had left her car back at the theater.

"She's staying with me," Lefty said blandly.

Marnie looked surprised, but she didn't utter any criticism. "Then I'll drive you both home" was all she said. This gave some support to David's impression that the two were only friends.

"We couldn't find an empty hotel room," Lefty explained. "No sweat. My sofa's comfortable. I often sleep on it myself. There's a window at the foot of it. Nice breeze. Strictly platonic," he added on the side to Marnie.

For a moment, Lisa had some hope Marnie might take pity on her and offer to put her up. She realized she was much too tired to begin the drive back to the inn. Marnie was bound to have a better place than Lefty, and it would be less disreputable to stay overnight with a woman. Marnie didn't ask her.

"How long are you staying?" was what she finally said.

"I'll be leaving early in the morning," Lisa told her.

Marnie drove them to Lefty's apartment, a dismal building that looked as if it should be condemned. "Come up for a drink?" Lefty invited Marnie.

"I wouldn't mind one before I go," Marnie decided.

Peeking at her watch, Lisa noticed it was midnight. She was weary and disappointed that the evening still wasn't over. What was the matter with Marnie that she didn't go home?

They all climbed the three flights of stairs to Lefty's apartment. The temperature rose as they climbed higher, till Lisa realized it was going to be like an oven inside. It was about what she imagined: a raggedy sofa, a chair, a pair of battered tables, a Woolworth's lamp, and a lot of clutter.

"You wouldn't believe the steal I got on this. A sublet, furnished," Lefty told them, then wandered into the kitchen.

"Places are so hard to get in New York," Marnie explained. "I'm going to call home and see if Cathy's all right."

Apparently Marnie knew the phone was in the bedroom, as that's where she headed. Lisa could hear her talking but didn't try to distinguish her words. Lefty came back with three cans of beer and no glasses. He pointed out to her how soft the sofa was, but if she didn't like it, she could have the bed and he'd be glad to take the sofa.

When he opened the window, there was a cooling breeze, and Lisa opted for the sofa. On the third floor, she didn't have to worry about anyone crawling in the window during the night.

"How's Cathy?" Lefty asked Marnie when she returned.

"She's sound asleep, but I told Mom I'd come right home. She worries about me," she added with a deprecating smile for the undue concern of mothers.

They drank their beer rather quickly. Before she left, Marnie turned to Lisa. "Oh, by the way, David had phoned Mom. He got your message when he went home, and he was wondering if she knew where you'd be. I guess it's too late to see him tonight. Why don't you give him a buzz in the morning? You have his number." Marnie looked at her with brightly curious eyes.

"Yes, I have it, thanks," Lisa said politely, but she didn't plan to phone him; she'd be leaving right after breakfast.

Lisa was surprised that Lefty bothered with the courtesy of walking Marnie to her car. It seemed unlike him, but then New York wasn't Spelling, and Marnie had parked a block away. Lisa was dead tired after her long day, and thoroughly despondent. She lay down on the sofa and closed her eyes, listening for Lefty's footsteps on the stairs outside. She didn't bother getting up when she heard him, but when the door opened, she peered from beneath her lashes and saw the shadowy outline of a man.

She knew at once it wasn't Lefty, and her first frightened thought was that a criminal had walked in, since she hadn't had the sense to lock the door. She sat bolt upright, her eyes wide open now, and found herself staring at a very angry David Spencer. There was a sharp crease between his brows and a grimace on his lips. He looked completely out of place in this shabby corner of the world, in his handsome summer suit, and with his sleek, careful barbering. All day, all evening—for a week—she'd been thinking of him, but in her fancy, he'd never looked like this, so angry.

"David!" she exclaimed in a squeak.

"Thanks for calling me!" was his first speech, delivered in a highly sarcastic tone.

"I called you the minute I got here!" she exclaimed self-righteously.

"You didn't get here very early, did you? Why the hell didn't you let me know yesterday, so I could have arranged something?" he demanded, his dark eyes shooting fire.

"Broken your *date*, you mean?" she snipped back.

"Yes, broken my date if you like. There are social functions that have to be attended. I don't live in a vacuum, and obviously *you* don't either," he accused, his voice loud.

Her own anger came bubbling up in defense. "It's too late to do anything about it now. It's past midnight, and I plan to go to bed," she replied, her chin tilted at a pugnacious angle.

"We'll talk about this in the car. Get your things. I'll drive you to your hotel," he ordered.

His imperative tone angered her further, and to have to admit she had no hotel room was a crushing embarrassment. She stifled these emotions and answered with a nonchalant toss of her head: "I'm staying with Lefty overnight."

"The hell you are!" he growled, a murderous glare boring into her. "You're not spending the night in this pigsty with that . . . that overgrown adolescent!" He looked around for her suitcase. It was on the floor by her feet, and he strode forward to pick it up.

"I prefer the pigsty to a park bench. I couldn't get a hotel room," she said, meeting his glare with an effort to be calm. She reached out and lifted her case from his fingers.

"Lisa, for God's sake!" he exclaimed impatiently. "If there's not a hotel room to be had—which I take leave to doubt—you can spend the night at my place."

"Kind of you to call me a liar!" she shot back with a defiant stare. "There's more than one kind of pigsty. Lefty's not the world's best housekeeper, but I prefer his physical pig style to the moral one you offer."

"I'm not offering you my *bed!*" he was quick to tell her. "For that matter, you can go to my mother's place. Marnie is just on her way home, so we won't disturb anyone," he pointed out.

Lisa was gratified at this belated offer of hospitality, but the manner of offering it made it impossible to accept. "I don't crash in uninvited," she said stiffly. "Marnie knew my situation, and she didn't offer me a room." She plunked her bag back on the floor.

"You're just looking for an excuse to stay here with *him*," he charged, pointing a condemning finger in her direction.

"*Excuse?*" she asked haughtily. "I don't need an excuse to visit an old friend, and I don't have to apologize to you either. You're nothing to me." Anger and embarrassment gnawed at her, just below the surface excitement of quarreling. She felt an ignoble urge to hurt her adversary.

"*Nothing!*" His tone betrayed surprise. For a moment he regarded her silently, but he didn't contradict her. He just continued staring, as though trying to come to some conclusion.

"Practically nothing," she modified in a carefully disinterested voice. "You asked me to give you a call when I came to New York, so I did. You happened to be busy. It's no big deal."

"It could have been, Lisa." And still those dark eyes examined her with that enigmatic look she didn't understand. "It could have been," he repeated, more softly.

"Then it's a pity you were busy," she answered curtly, her voice curiously flat. She had to hold herself under tight control, or all her frustration would come pouring out. All the hours of waiting, hoping to see him, the impatience and disappointment, and now finally to be found in this sleazy atmosphere—it was too much to bear.

"I asked you to phone me when you were coming to New York. Naturally I meant before, to give me a little notice."

"*Naturally*," she agreed, mocking him with a smile, "but it didn't occur to me you led such an active social life. I don't suppose *one* evening's notice would have been enough in any case, and I only decided yesterday. You probably have your calendar booked up weeks in advance."

His expression was no longer enigmatic. It had settled down to a blighting stare. "No, *months*," he corrected, "but unlike you, I would have squeezed *one hour* of my precious time free for you."

"One hour doesn't strike me as a big deal. You're obviously too busy to bother with me," she answered, tossing her shoulders to show her lack of interest.

"That has a familiar ring!"

"*I* was busy with *work*," she pointed out.

"What do you think *I* was doing?"

"I think you were out with a woman. Offices aren't open for business at midnight." She heard the jealous, accusing accents in her voice and tried to hold on to her control.

"*I* have friends, too," he said reasonably. "We've agreed excuses aren't necessary for visiting friends. When the visit lasts till morning, however, even the most unsuspecting will become a little suspicious. Let me take you to

mother's, Lisa. I can't believe you want to spend the night
here." His eyes traveled around the dingy room as he
finished speaking, and his lips thinned in distaste.

Though she blushed because of the looks of the place, she
answered calmly, "I take my friends as I find them. If you
don't like the place, you can leave."

"Not without you," he replied, equally calm, but determined.

"I plan to stay. As you said, I'm independent. I'm in the
habit of looking after myself."

"I'm aware of your efforts in that direction, but you do a
lousy job," he said bluntly, derision tautening his facial
muscles into a sneering mask. "You nearly ran that inn into
the ground, and now you're starting on yourself. Worn to a
bone. You look like death on wheels, Lisa." His scowl
softened gradually as he spoke, but the slur on her looks
was a fresh blow to her pride.

"Lefty doesn't mind," she told him with a bright smile.
While he stood staring at her, she reached down and
unfastened her case, pulled out a filmy blue nightie, and
shook it out before placing it on the sofa.

At the sight of it, David's whole body stiffened. For
about thirty seconds he just looked. Then he marched
forward, caught a glimpse of the phone through the
bedroom doorway, went to it, and called his mother. His
loud voice was perfectly audible from the sofa.

"I have an unexpected guest, Mother. I'm bringing her to
you for the night. All right?" he asked, but his tone was
dictatorial. There was a slight pause while his mother
replied. "Very soon," he said, and hung up.

He might have his mother under his thumb, but Lisa was
more determined than ever to follow her own plan. When
David returned to the living room, he picked up the case,

threw the blue nightie into it, and said, "Come on. We're leaving now." His tone was sharp, commanding, and his lips were thin with anger.

She sat down, crossed her legs, and leaned back against the sofa with an attitude of comfort, though every nerve and muscle in her body was taut with tension. "I'm staying. Are you going to steal my nightie? I'll just have to do without it. But it's a warm night. We—*I* won't mind." She looked at him, a bold, challenging look.

He took one step toward her, dropped the case, and reached for her. "If you touch me, I'll scream my head off," she warned.

He stopped, looked at her for a moment, with the anger and determination in his eyes changing to disgust. "You win. You're not worth that much trouble," he said in a mocking manner. He shrugged his shoulders and walked out of the room, out of her life, and didn't even slam the door.

She crumpled in a heap as soon as he was gone, like a rag doll. She was relieved to be alone, and was momentarily overwhelmed at the outcome of the visit. Why had she ever undertaken this misbegotten trip? So long anticipated with joy, it had been a total calamity. There hadn't been a moment's pleasure in it since she parked her van in front of the theater. And now this *disaster*.

She dragged herself up from the sofa and turned to examine herself in the mirror hanging above it. Her hair was unkempt from the humidity and completely tangled, but the disheveled hair was only the topping. Her whole appearance was wretched. Her old blouse and skirt were all wrinkled, and there was even a blob of chili sauce on the blouse from the restaurant. Her face was pale, and there were circles etched under her eyes from weeks of worry, aggravated by the strain of driving half the day. The endless waiting to hear from David had added its toll. She looked like a ghost. When had she got so thin? She used to have nice round cheeks. God, no wonder he said she looked like death. She wouldn't even make an attractive corpse.

The heat and disorder of Lefty's apartment added to her discomfort. She wanted to take a shower, to wash the travel stains down the drain, and with it the gnawing regret at having finally lost David for good. He'd probably spent the evening with some highly polished and attractive woman, then had come and found her looking like this. And shacking up for the night with Lefty Spinner in the bargain—that's what he thought, and she'd taken care to see he did think it. He was right. She was a fool, a worse fool than he could possibly know.

She wandered disconsolately to the bathroom, but the tub was grimy. She doubted if it had been cleaned since Lefty moved in. She was too tired to clean it, and too repulsed to use it in its present state, so she went back to the sofa and sat down, waiting for Lefty to come in and go to bed, so she could cry in private. Her jaw ached with the desire to cry. Again she regretted having made this awful journey. Let others love New York. She hated it with all her heart, because she hated herself.

She was on the sofa, hugging her knees to her chest when Lefty sauntered in a moment later.

"Old Dave's in one lousy mood. What did you do to him?" he asked with mild curiosity.

"Nothing much. I just said I was staying here with you. He probably misunderstood it," she said.

"Some people have minds like sewers. That guy never did like me. He thinks I'm after Marnie's money. No way. Lefty travels alone. The Marnie thing—strictly platonic, if you're interested," he mentioned, and flopped into the chair.

"You look beat, kid" was his next effort at conversation. "Ever since you got here. You're missing Lefty at the inn, huh?" he asked.

"We all miss you, Lefty," she told him. "The whole staff send their regards."

"I miss them, too, Boss Lady. More than I show. There's one great big heart beating in here," he told her, thumping his chest with a closed fist. "Hey, why don't you tell old Uncle Lefty what's really bugging you? Life's for sharing," he said simply.

Suddenly she knew she wanted to talk. For too long she'd kept all her troubles locked in her own breast, unable to talk with Leo about bothersome problems because of his health. And Lefty was a harmless confidant. There was no vice in him.

"Paradise Inn is getting me down," she began, and it all came spilling out. Lefty was comforting and sympathetic, a good listener. He was willing to share her pain, but of course he couldn't do anything concrete to help. She told him her plans to sell. "I just don't think I can hack it another year," she said sadly.

"A wise decision, Lisa Baby," he agreed, reverting to his first choice of title for her. "There's a time to fight, and a time to throw in the towel. A time to sow and a time to reap," he added vaguely. "It's every man for himself. There's a jungle out there. Gee, it'll be sad to think there's no Paradise Inn to go back to, though. What'll you do?" he asked with interest.

"I have no idea. Invest the money and get a job, I think."

"If you'd care to invest in a play, I have a line on a very hot property. An underground film," he added, peering to see if that elicited any interest.

"Too risky," she said at once.

"I might be able to get you into something. I have a few contacts in this business now," he offered half-heartedly. "The downtrodden look is catching on in commercials. Housewife stuff—detergents, floor wax . . ."

This unflattering assessment of her looks wasn't challenged, but it was noted for future correction, nevertheless.

They talked for three hours. Lefty made a large pot of tea, and they sat together, discussing old times and the uncertain future. It was better than crying alone in the dark. There was a hint of rose in the sky when they finally called it a night. Lisa didn't even bother undressing. She just lay on the sofa and dozed off for a couple of hours. At six o'clock she crept quietly into the bathroom to splash water on her face and brush her hair. She left Lefty a note thanking him, then found her way back to the theater to pick up her van. The streets were nearly empty, and the air hadn't begun to turn hot yet.

She drove out of the city before stopping for breakfast at a highway restaurant. Her eyes were gritty from lack of sleep, and her heart was heavy. The trip had been worse than futile. It had been a humiliation. David wasn't going to be a white knight, rescuing her from the morass she'd worked herself into. In fact, David had a girl friend, which had, strangely, never occurred to her. So that was that. She'd have to get busy and take care of herself, as she always had. And she'd take care of her looks, too. Nobody would hire a bedraggled, despondent woman. It wasn't the end of her life, just the end of a dream.

It was the second dream that had died on her that summer and the experience didn't become any less painful with repetition. What she needed now was a new dream, but the ghost of the old haunted her. She saw David's face in the green-clad hills of the countryside, heard the echo of his infectious, debonair laugh in the silence, and felt as lonesome as a brand-new widow.

Chapter Nine

The trip was such a fiasco that Lisa was actually happy to get back to her prison. She showered and changed into a light cotton dress just in time to join Leo for lunch.

"I didn't expect you back so early. Did you have a good time?" he asked, wreathed in smiles.

She had to put on a smile, too, and pretend she had had a perfectly delightful visit. Leo didn't know how strongly David had been featured in her plans, so she could skip over that lightly. He'd been busy, she said. She spared him the tale of her night with Lefty and made much of the play. They laughed together over it, and Leo prophesied they'd see Lefty back by autumn.

"He'll blow in about the time we don't need him, the end of September," Leo said. "We don't have anything booked past September, except a couple of Thanksgiving weekend guests."

"Yes, the autumn bookings have fallen off this year," she said with a worried frown.

"We can use a bit of peace and quiet," he said contentedly, but Leo didn't know the disastrous state of the books. In his illness, she'd spared him the truth. It was still too early to announce her plan to sell, but she began introducing the idea to get him used to it.

"Sometimes I'd like to just go away and forget all about the inn. Remember that chicken farm you used to talk about, Leo?"

"It was a gentleman's hobby farm. I want a cow and a pair of pigs, too," he told her and discussed that for a while, with enough enthusiasm that she felt he might be happy on a little farm.

She continued about her usual business the next days, but she spent her evenings bent over the books, figuring, planning, wondering if it was worth continuing. She had cut every corner known to geometry but still couldn't see the possibility of making a substantial profit. Scraping along was the best she could do, and that was only if no major catastrophe occurred. When the catastrophe finally did come, she threw in the towel and gave up.

It was really only a minor major catastrophe, but it was enough to dip her into the red. Of all the things that could have gone wrong with the inn proper, it was the old van breaking down on her that did it. How could you run a country inn without any transportation into the town for the dozens of emergencies that arose every week? You couldn't, and the van couldn't be repaired. It just died of old age—died in service, like a good soldier.

Lisa had driven into Spelling one sultry Saturday morning to pick up the fresh produce for the weekend at the local farmers' market. The back of the van was full of baskets of plump, ripe peaches and vegetables. When she got behind the wheel to drive home, the engine wouldn't start. The mechanic from the closest garage shook his head and said he'd have to tow it into the garage to analyze the fault. "It's just plum worn out" was his verdict an hour later. There were so many parts worn out or on the verge of going that it was no longer worth fixing.

The taxi home cost ten dollars, and Lisa had to add a hefty tip for the driver's help in transporting her produce to the inn. To buy even a secondhand replacement would cost a couple of thousand. That evening she told Leo her decision. He was distraught and offered to lend her his life savings. Dear, foolhardy Leo, willing to throw good money after bad to keep her dream alive. But the dream had lost its luster. She felt a kind of euphoria at having finally taken the inevitable decision. She wrote to cancel the Thanksgiving reservations and would accept no more.

She called the Spelling real estate agent out to the inn for an assessment and listed it for sale. No sign was posted till the last guest had departed at the end of August. The agent thought her asking price a little high, but she told him she had already refused that same offer earlier in the season, so he accepted it. David's offer had been generous, then, she noted to herself, always with that needle of regret that she'd refused it.

She worked out the arithmetic in her head. She'd give Leo one-third of the sale price and let him buy his farm. She'd invest the rest for her own future, keeping enough to live on till she got a job. The whole world lay before her. She didn't have to live in Spelling if she didn't want to. She could go to New York or Rome or Paris. She enjoyed a brief, mental tour of the world, but when she came back to reality, she realized that her home and her heart belonged right here where she was, in this general vicinity of the Poconos.

All the activity served an added purpose in that it helped deflect her thoughts from David Spencer. She couldn't ignore that his ski lodge was rapidly taking form on the other side of the mountain. The hills rang with the sound of large construction equipment coming and going. She often thought of the magical afternoon in the woods with David. What would have happened if she hadn't had to rush back to work? And where, she wondered, was David now? What was he doing—and with whom?

Lefty sent her a postcard but spoke only of himself. *Tossed Salad* was cancelled. He'd be back "home" in September. She wrote to tell him that the inn was for sale. He was welcome to stay till he found something else, but she couldn't afford to pay him a salary. She could almost hear his answer. "No sweat, Boss Lady. Lefty isn't asking for any handouts."

Offers on the inn were as slow and as scarce as she'd feared they would be. It was too big for a private home, and really too small for a profitable hotel. She just sat tight and waited, trimming her sails to the loss of income. In order to live, she advertised the dining room in Spelling and began serving evening dinners to anyone who would bother driving the twelve miles. When the last honeymoon guest had departed, the signs were posted on the gates, announcing the sale. It was a forlorn sight that always pulled at her heartstrings.

All that month she didn't actually see David, but she heard indirectly of him once. On the day her final honeymooners took their departure, Mrs. Latham said, "Oh, by the way, there's a message for you at the switchboard. David Spencer is at the hotel in Spelling and wants you to call him."

An unquenchable spurt of hope flared in her breast. "What time did he phone?" she asked, already turning toward her office to have privacy for the call.

"Half an hour ago. I looked all over for you, but Leo thought you were out."

"I was in the attic, sorting through junk to throw out. I'll phone him now." Her heart fluttered anxiously as she placed the call. Remembering their last meeting, she knew there would be some initial embarrassment but was ready to face it. A dozen times she'd wished for a chance to explain that unfortunate evening in New York.

The hotel was very sorry, but Mr. Spencer had checked out a short time ago. They offered to give her his New York number, but Lisa just hung up. What could he have wanted? Not a date, apparently, as he was leaving right away for home. Perhaps he'd just been calling to say hello, or maybe he was giving a message from Lefty, through Marnie. She wouldn't call him in New York. That looked as if she placed too much importance on his call. He spent a lot of time in Spelling, and if it was anything important he'd call again next week. "Important" to Lisa had only one meaning— that he wanted to see her.

That Saturday Lisa threw a party for her employees. The maids and waiters served themselves from a long smorgasbord table temporarily arranged for the occasion. It was a happy event, but with an edge of sadness to it. The end of an era. On Sunday morning, she awoke and for about one minute frowned at the sun, streaming in her window.

Then reality dawned on her, that today she didn't have to get up at seven and begin her duties. There were only Leo and herself in the building. How lonesome it felt.

The chef, Herbert, would handle dinner, and the local summer help would serve it. Leo was around to take any calls for reservations, so she would actually get to swim in her own pool, to walk through Ophelia's Garden, and gather some roses if she felt like it.

But before any of this, she could just close her eyes and sleep till she felt like getting up. When she next opened her eyes, it was nine o'clock, and she was thoroughly rested. Leo had already eaten and was in the kitchen. He insisted on making her bacon and eggs, which she took out to the back patio to eat in splendid solitude, with only the birds and squirrels for company. The sadness, the sense of loss, was with her, but to think of not getting an offer at all was worse. Would she *never* get a buyer for the inn?

It was too nice a day to worry about it. She walked through her gardens, through the mini orchard, noticing that the apples were coming along nicely. At eleven, she put on her bathing suit and lounged in a chair by the pool, swimming when she felt like it, all alone with her memories, till she became bored with their company and went back to the inn to find something to do. The early afternoon was idled away in selecting items she wanted to take with her when she sold the place.

"Why aren't you out enjoying yourself on a nice day like this?" Mrs. Latham chided when she came to set up the tables for dinner. "You've earned a good rest, my girl."

But "rest" was just another word for nothing to do. Lisa had already begun answering employment ads in the paper. She wasn't accustomed to handling leisure. It was stultifying. At six she dressed in a long flowered skirt and black top to act as hostess for the dinner. It was better than sitting alone in her room.

There was a respectable showing of guests. Quickly calculating her night's profit, Lisa was satisfied. At eight-thirty, she was about to vacate her post, as the flow of guests had stopped. She went to the front door and peeked out to ensure that no one else was coming. Her hand flew to her mouth, and a low gasp escaped from her lips. David Spencer was walking along the path to the door, accompanied by an elegant-looking woman. She wasn't a young woman, but not old either. Lisa estimated her to be about David's age. Her black hair was pulled back in a chic roll, and the brightly colored dress was of a floating, sheer material that appeared out of place in this simple country setting.

But it was the face that caught Lisa's attention. She was attractive without being at all beautiful. She had dark eyes and sharp features, rather French looking. A bright flow of chatter was coming from the woman as she looked all around at the rose garden, and the quaint half-timbered and brick front of the inn. David was pointing out the leaded windows to her, with his hand on her elbow.

Lisa darted back quickly to her post and composed her face to bland politeness when they came in, but her heart was racing violently, and her color was high.

"Hello, Lisa," David said, walking forward to shake her hand. His voice was friendly but impersonal, with no trace of the violent anger displayed at their last meeting. "I heard last week that the inn is up for sale, and I came to bid it *adieu*. I'd like you to meet an old friend of mine from New York. I brought Miss Milstrom with me. She's interested in these old inns."

"How do you do?" Lisa said, shaking the woman's

hand. And while she said the polite, welcoming things, her mind was on David and his arrival. Had he come all the way from New York just to have dinner and show his friend the inn? It was a long trip for such a slight reward. Or was it just the tail end of an afternoon's drive? They'd been out together—did David happen to mention he knew this out-of-the-way place she might find amusing? Yes, that was more like it.

"A beautiful part of the country," Miss Milstrom said. "David showed me his ski lodge. It'll be a delightful place to go on winter weekends."

Ah, so *that* was it! He'd brought Miss Milstrom, who soon asked Lisa to call her Nadia, to see his ski resort. That made sense. But bringing the woman still made real sense only if she meant a great deal to him. During the five minutes they chatted together, Lisa found it entirely possible that Nadia was the woman Marnie had called David's girl friend. She was lively, good-natured, and intelligent. It was hard to dislike her, and when one can't dislike a rival, then the rival must be a charmer indeed.

The early arrivals began to leave shortly after David and Nadia were served dinner. City hours for dining hadn't caught on in Spelling. Lisa stayed at her post to say good-bye to them in the hope of luring them back again. She was aware that she was directly in David's line of vision and knew that he often glanced at her. It made her nervous, and she decided to leave the dining room. She went to her office to do the paperwork involved in running the dining room.

She left the door ajar, and when she sat down she found she was too upset to work. She just sat, looking out at her old friend, the groaning pine tree. In her mind, she was climbing it as she had done as a child. It brought a misty smile to her face. She was jolted back to reality by a light tap at her door.

"What is it?" she asked, turning to see who it was, expecting Leo. "David!" she exclaimed, staring. A moment of panic descended on her at the thought of being alone with him. Had he come to say something that couldn't be said in front of other people?

"Did I frighten you? Sorry." He spoke in a natural, easy way, but there was some latent tension or uncertainty in his face. He looked at her too long and too hard for comfort. "Nadia and I were wondering if you'd join us for coffee and a liqueur. Dinner was delightful, by the way. I see you've dispensed with both the bubbly and the pink whipped cream. Would it be in poor taste for me to congratulate you?" This reference to former times disconcerted her. It was said in a dulcet joking voice designed for that purpose, she thought, but she hid her feelings.

"I wonder that you chose my restaurant, when you had such a poor opinion of the menu," she replied, aiming a questioning eye at him. It was reassuring to watch his composure slip.

He seemed quite definitely ill at ease, now that he was alone with her. "Dinner wasn't the only reason for coming," he replied.

"I shouldn't think it was worth a trip from New York," she agreed. "What was the other reason?"

"I wanted to see you," he said uncertainly.

Lisa found she enjoyed being on the attack for a change. She didn't know why David was uncomfortable, but she knew very well that he was. "It was kind of you to worry about me. You'll be relieved to see I haven't toppled into my grave yet. You mentioned I was in danger of it the last time we met," she reminded him. She was happy to know she now looked much better.

"I said a lot of foolish things," he admitted. "But you weren't quite truthful with *me* either. You gave me no idea you were in such desperate financial trouble."

"Why should I? I hardly have to remind you that you were of no help to me in that regard."

A frustrated glare was his first response to her jibe. "I didn't come here to argue," he said, reining in his temper.

"No, presumably you came to have dinner and to see me. You've had dinner, and you've seen me. Was there anything else?"

"Yes. I've already asked you if you'd join Nadia and me for coffee. She'll be wondering what's taking so long," he pointed out.

"Then I'll let you go now, and deliver my regrets," she said, pulling a sheet of paper toward her, as though hard at work. She didn't want to think about why David brought out the worst in her; she simply waited to hear his retreating footsteps. But when all she heard was an ominous silence, she raised her head. Anger and frustration were visible in every rigid line of his body.

"I wish you'd reconsider your answer," he said. "Of course, if you feel ill at ease with Miss Milstrom, I'm sure she'll understand."

"Why should I?" Lisa asked sharply, disliking the intimation that Miss Milstrom was so far above her socially that she'd be squirming in her shoes.

"You shouldn't. The only other reason I can think of is that it's *my* presence you object to. I came to offer an olive branch, Lisa. I don't see why we can't be . . . *friends?*"

He tilted his head and gave one of his charming smiles, while his questioning tone imbued the word *friend* with some ambiguity. There was even a tinge of challenge in his expression.

To imply that she was ill at ease with him was even more galling than fearing Miss Milstrom. "I suppose I can spare a few minutes," she said, then rose reluctantly from her chair.

With the barrier of the desk removed, she felt strangely vulnerable. She experienced a fear—or was it a hope?—that he'd touch her, perhaps kiss her, or try to. But he just stood aside and let her precede him to the door. Whatever his real motive in asking for this meeting with Miss Milstrom, Lisa refused to be condescended to, or made fun of. She'd failed in her business, but it wasn't all her fault. The circumstances had been partly to blame. And as to the maudlin decor, what else would be expected at a honeymoon hotel? She'd be sure to let the sophisticated Miss Milstrom know her own taste was quite different. She was unaware of David's scrutiny as these thoughts flitted through her head.

"We don't plan to *beat* you, you know," he said when she reached the door. "Much as you deserve it," he added. It was the only voluntary reference he made to that night in New York. She cast an uncertain glimpse at him, and he dropped the subject instantly.

"Nadia's very nice. I think you'll like her," he said in a natural way.

"I'm sure I shall," she answered.

Lisa sat between David and Nadia, sipping coffee, and feeling like an intruder. Her main thought was an excuse to escape.

"Why did you decide to sell the inn, Lisa?" Nadia

asked, her dark eyes alive with interest. She was one of those people who was interested in everything and everyone, Lisa decided. That was her charm.

"Simple economics," Lisa confessed. "I wasn't making any money. I plan to unload it and do something else. It costs a fortune to keep up an old barn of a place like this. The plumbing is on its last legs, the roof could use some work . . ."

"Lisa made a great many improvements a few years ago," David said, interrupting her with a compelling glare that she couldn't understand. "There's a beautiful pool out back, and of course the rose gardens in front are lovely."

"You can't eat roses," Lisa said with a disparaging shrug.

"The roses are beautiful," Nadia agreed, with a knowing little smile at David. "You were saying about the roof needing work, Lisa," she went on, turning back to her hostess.

"The roof, the windows, even the floor here in the dining room isn't quite even," Lisa told her.

"These old places can be a nuisance," Nadia said consolingly.

"The property itself is lovely," David said firmly, almost angrily. "And the new fixtures installed in the Imperial Suite are quite . . . er . . . distinctive," he added to Nadia.

Lisa tossed her head back and laughed. "Beautiful, if you have a taste for hearts and flowers! He's making fun of me," Lisa explained, trying for an air of sophistication to match Nadia's. "A heart-shaped tub for two, with pink ceramic tiles. I wish I had the money I wasted on that monstrosity. But for a honeymoon hotel, you know, it seemed appropriate."

Nadia joined in the laughter. "I'd *adore* seeing it! Would it be possible, now that you have no guests?"

"Certainly. I'm afraid my renovations are enough to put off any sane buyer. But you never know," Lisa said.

"It's really quite charming," David insisted.

"You'd never guess to look at him that David is a romantic, would you?" Nadia asked playfully. "I hear it makes an excellent bed," she said with a teasing smile. Lisa realized there was a close friendship between these two, since he'd even told her that.

"He complained of the noise when he slept in it," Lisa answered, assuming Nadia was aware of all the intricacies of that visit.

"I shouldn't think it would squeak at least," Nadia said with a frown.

"No, it was the plumbing, actually," David said, with a private smile for Lisa, "but I believe that was rectified."

"What do you do for a living, Nadia?" Lisa asked rather hastily, deeming it time to change the subject.

"I do ceramics," she said proudly. "I have a line of ceramic jewelry—pendants, brooches. Perhaps you've heard of the Milstrom line?"

"I don't believe so," Lisa answered.

"I sell them in boutiques in New York. I also do ornamental pottery. I'm working on a foolproof glaze. Glazing is the most uncertain step," she explained.

"You sound like an expert," Lisa said, impressed.

"Well, I'm in *Who's Who*," Nadia admitted modestly. "I give classes to a few gifted students in New York."

"It's too bad I hadn't known you sooner. I could have had you design me a souvenir piece to sell at my inn."

"I do a lot of that sort of thing, actually," Nadia replied, and went on with a few examples of her work.

"Would you like to go up and see the *pièce de résistance* now?" Lisa asked when they had finished their drinks.

"We should really go out and look around the back gardens first," David mentioned.

"Silly! It's pitch dark," Nadia told him with a playful pat on the hand. Lisa took note of the familiar gesture. Surely no one but a lover would do that.

"We can come back tomorrow and see the outside," Nadia decided.

Lisa looked at her with increasing curiosity. Come all the way from New York to look at a few acres of garden? "We're staying at the hotel in Spelling," Nadia added nonchalantly.

"Oh, I see," Lisa said, still holding her smile, but it had become rigid around the edges. David glared at Nadia as though he'd like to hit her.

"Shall we go upstairs now?" he asked. There was a sharp edge to his voice, and a sharp look to Lisa, who refused to meet it.

"Oh, this is priceless!" Nadia exclaimed as she stood at the door of the Imperial Suite. "Where on *earth* did you find wallpaper with actual hearts and flowers on it? And cupids!" A tinkle of silver laughter hung on the air.

Gazing at the room, Lisa realized fully that it was indeed done in mawkish taste. The fragile spell was broken. "There's a commercial decorating house that does specialty lines," she told Nadia. "They do bars and clubs and things. The infamous tub is in here," she said, and walked to open the bathroom door. A pair of brass-plated cupids cavorted merrily, serving as taps in the whirlpool tub. What had once struck her as cute now looked decidedly tawdry.

"I'm dying to try it. Could we stay here overnight,

David? Oh, it's really you I should be asking, Lisa,'' Nadia said, turning to her hostess.

"I'm afraid we're closed for overnight guests," Lisa said firmly. "I haven't any staff to tend the rooms now."

"Could I just take a peek around some other rooms while we're here?" she pressed on.

"They're just ordinary rooms," Lisa told her. "The Romeo-and-Juliet suite has a balcony, of course."

That also had to be seen. There were more jokes about it. Lisa held her temper, but she was becoming annoyed with Nadia and David. David sensed her jagged temper and said, "We'd better go now, Nadia. Thanks so much for the tour, Lisa."

"It was my pleasure," she said, not even trying to sound sincere.

"May I see the gardens tomorrow?" Nadia asked shamelessly.

"You're welcome to drive out and look around. I'm not sure I'll be here, but I'll tell Leo to make you welcome," she said. She would be here, of course. Where could she go, without even a car? But she wouldn't listen to any more of this woman's sly putdowns. She felt defensive about her inn, like a mother with an unattractive child. It was all right for her to say the decor was maudlin, but she didn't enjoy to hear others laugh at it.

They went downstairs to take their leave of each other. At the door, Nadia said, "What do you plan to do when you leave, Lisa?"

"I'll get a job," she answered briefly.

"You should speak to David about it. He'll be hiring help for the ski lodge. Why don't you hire her to run the lodge, David?" Nadia suggested brightly.

Although it was an obvious notion, it hadn't occurred to Lisa, and she thought from the look of surprise on David's face that he hadn't thought of it either. Of course, she wasn't qualified to manage such a large operation, but she might find some less grand job there.

"Oh, I wouldn't be qualified to *run* it," Lisa said, but she looked with interest to see how David reacted to the idea of having her work there in some other capacity.

He gave one of his debonair laughs at the very idea. "No, I prefer not to go bankrupt."

His thoughtless joke was like a slap in the face. Coming on top of the unpleasant visit, it was all she could do to hold in the tears. Anger rose up, and she longed to retaliate, but her throat was locked. No words came. David looked at her, and the laugh faded. "Not that you've declared bankruptcy," he added quickly.

"Lisa would make a charming hostess," Nadia said, diplomatically trying to cover David's gaffe.

But even this job, so much lower than her former one, met with no pleasure from him. "That would be underemploying her talents."

"You're right," Nadia agreed at once, "but there must be some position suitable to her experience."

"A manager has already been hired," David said brusquely. "He's in charge of personnel. Naturally, Lisa is free to apply if she's interested." Throughout this exchange, it was only Nadia who actually looked at Lisa. David spoke of her as though she weren't present.

He spoke as though it were all beyond his power, but he only had to say the word, and she'd be given any job he mentioned. No, Lisa knew he just didn't want to hire her.

When Lisa managed to swallow the lump in her throat,

she said to Nadia, purposely ignoring David, "He's afraid I'd paint the place pink, you see."

"Oh, the decorating has already been done, and it's gorgeous," Nadia told her.

Even this caused a wince of pain, as Lisa realized that he had taken Nadia to see it, and not her.

They soon left, and Lisa went upstairs to her own rooms to think over the unexpected visit. Why had they come? Why had David brought that woman here to laugh at her establishment? Oh, she had joined in the laughter herself, but somewhere inside there was a dull ache, a sadness to see her life's work held up to scorn. It began to look like nothing else but a sadistic form of revenge David was taking, bringing his friends here to laugh and mock.

She remembered, too, his reluctance to offer her a job at his ski lodge. Then she finally allowed herself to think about what was really bothering her. David and Nadia in that hotel in Spelling together, now . . .

How did they have the nerve to ask to come back tomorrow and laugh at her gardens? She'd said they could come, but she wouldn't see them. If she had to hide in the cellar, she would *not* listen to any more of their jokes.

It was hot in the bedroom. She put on a cotton nightgown and went out to Juliet's balcony for a breath of air. A fat orangy-yellow moon hung low in the sky. The harvest moon, her father used to call it. It was harvest time in the countryside, but there was no harvest for her, after all her work. It was beginning to look dreadfully as though she'd be here through the winter. Maybe it wouldn't be so bad. She could go over to the ski lodge and learn to ski. But first she'd have to find a job, and that meant a car, since she'd be living here in the country.

She could type and do bookkeeping, or maybe work as an operator for Bell. There had to be something she could do to keep body and soul together. And what about Leo? She had to see that he got *some* money. She sat on the little wrought-iron bench, rubbing her brow in worry. Leo had suggested an auction sale of the furnishings and dining room gear. Maybe she should do it. If she didn't get an offer by the end of September, she'd contact the local auctioneer. She'd have the desperate experience of standing, watching strangers bid on her memories. Going, going, gone.

Chapter Ten

Monday was known locally as such a poor night for dining out that most of the restaurants were closed, and Lisa followed their example. She had no duties on Monday, and as the weather was chilly for swimming, she took the bus into Spelling and went to the employment agency to fill in an application. It was like a journey into the past, trying to remember in what year she had graduated from high school, and all her work history over the intervening years. Most of it was at the inn, but she had served in such varied capacities that she hardly knew what facet of her experience to emphasize. What she was qualified for was running a small hotel, and even that she had done so badly she managed to run it into the ground. It was a demoralizing morning.

She felt demolished when she left the place. It was just noon, and with the next bus home leaving at two-thirty, she had a long wait. She *must* get a car, something to get her to town, even if it was a wreck. She stood at the door of the agency, deciding where to have lunch. Casey's had good smoked-meat sandwiches and cheesecake, and it wasn't too far to walk. She turned right and took three paces, before a low-slung white car pulled in beside her. From the corner of her eye, she saw a man at the wheel and was more flattered than offended that someone was trying to pick her up. It renewed her confidence in her appearance. She'd set him down gently, whoever he was.

"Going my way?" a man's voice asked. She recognized it as David's at once. Looking into the darker interior of the car, she saw a flash of white teeth and a pair of sunglasses. Her heart lurched.

"What a letdown!" she exclaimed, smiling. "Here I thought someone was trying to pick me up."

"I'm someone," he pointed out. "Can I give you a lift?"

"I'm just going to the restaurant for lunch—it's only a block," she said, not mentioning that she had lost her van.

"Are you meeting anyone?" he persisted.

"No," she said reluctantly, fearing he was on his way to pick up Nadia. She could do without another session with that woman.

"Good. Hop in and I'll join you, if you don't mind."

As a car behind him honked, she opened the door and got in. "Is it Casey's you're headed to?" he asked.

She nodded affirmatively.

"Good pastrami," he said, then pulled back into the line of traffic.

He parked on the street and they found a seat in the busy little restaurant, where businessmen and businesswomen made up the noon clientele. "What brings you to town?" David asked, picking up the menu.

"Business," she said vaguely. "Where's Nadia today?"

"She's out scouring the art shops, I believe. I was at the ski site this morning, and she mentioned doing the stores to see how she likes . . ." He came to a conscious stop. There was a furtive look in his eyes, as though he'd said more than he meant to. "How she likes the wares," he finished, and rushed on immediately to talk about their lunch.

"We must have a draft beer with that. A pastrami without a beer is illegal," he said in his old, light-hearted way.

"Fine, I don't want to get arrested. I'll have a beer, too," she said, but she was mentally finishing that interrupted sentence. "Doing the stores to see how she likes them" was obviously what he meant to say. But "how she likes them" suggested more than one fleeting trip. It sounded almost as though Nadia meant to move into the neighborhood. The ski lodge was the next thing that flashed into her mind. David had brought her down here to have a look at the lodge, presumably to see how she liked it, too. But why would a potter from New York—with students in New York, in fact—be moving to the Poconos? Did David intend to move here? He was on the Board of Directors of the Spelling bank, so maybe with the lodge here, too, he was thinking of moving. And bringing Nadia with him.

She carefully threaded her conversation toward learning if this was true. "How is the lodge coming along?" was a natural question.

"Super. It'll be open this winter. They've planted rye or something on the slopes, so there'll be a root system there for the snow to grab onto. Otherwise, the hill might collapse," he told her. "It'll look better in the summers, too, with a green covering."

"You wouldn't want to make it look as though the mountain had been strip-mined," she agreed. "Will you be

able to spend much time at the lodge, living in New York?''
she asked blandly.

"Between you and me and the pastrami," he said,
leaning his head close to hers, "I plan to move in
permanently. I've got a suite for myself in the penthouse.
What a view!" His eyes glowed with enthusiasm.

"A studio?" she asked casually.

"Oh, no, a full apartment. A kitchen, living room,
office, bedrooms. I couldn't ask . . . I mean, I couldn't live
in one room," he finished, in confusion.

She mentally reworked another unfinished sentence. "I
couldn't ask Nadia to live in one room."

He rattled on to cover the little lapse. "You must come
over and see it, Lisa. I think you'd like it. I'll keep up the
New York place, as I have to spend a day or so a week there
for business, but I hope to phase that out gradually."

"And you're actually thinking of moving to the Poconos
to *live?*" she asked, stricken to the heart.

"I'm going to give it a try," he said uncertainly. "Nadia
says I'm a New York hick and won't be happy away from
concrete and crowds."

"Does Nadia like the country?" she asked.

"She's always loved it," he assured her.

The sandwich arrived, and though Casey was famous for
his pastrami, it went unappreciated by Lisa. She could have
been eating sawdust for all she noticed. David was moving
to the lodge, and Nadia was out cruising the town to see if
she could be happy here. Marriage then, obviously.

"Were you at the real estate agent's in town? Was that
your business?" David asked later.

"No, I was at the employment agency. I'm looking for a
job," she said, hoping he might have reconsidered. They'd

be hiring dozens of people at the lodge. It would be an interesting, exciting place to work, and she had plenty of experience.

"Have you sold the inn, then?" he asked, surprised. "I hope you didn't settle for too little."

"I haven't even had a serious nibble," she admitted. "I need a job to see me through till I do sell. The problem is rather urgent, actually," she added, gazing at him all the while. "I won't run the evening dinners in the winter. No one would come. I have to find something by winter."

It was practically a request, and still the expected offer wasn't forthcoming. He lifted his eyes to hers, saw the desperate hope shining, and looked away. His lack of response angered her, but she couldn't afford anger. She had to be conciliatory.

"They didn't hold out much hope at the agency," she added. Surely if there was a drop of charity, or caring, in his body, he'd offer something. "I don't know *what* I'll do," she added, and waited. He couldn't ignore that.

"Just how bad is the situation? You mentioned the word 'desperate,'?" he reminded her.

"I wasn't exaggerating. And I have Leo to worry about, too," she replied. David was playing with his napkin distractedly. It wasn't like him to be so fidgety, ill at ease.

"I'm sure you'll find something," he said, just glancing at her. It was a wary look.

"I wish I could share your optimism. This wasn't my first attempt to find work." There was nothing more she could do but beg. She even toyed with the idea of doing that, but if he refused . . . No, she'd gone as far as she could with hinting, and she would *not* beg, not if she had to live on a bone. While the resentment began to build up at his indifference, she saw that he was struggling with something. A frown of indecision was on his face, flickering, still with that wary light in his eyes.

After an embarrassingly long pause, he spoke. "I don't want to offend you, Lisa, but . . ."

"I know," she said curtly, cutting him off. "You don't think I'd make a suitable employee for your slick lodge. You're probably right."

A flash of anger leaped across his face. "Damn it! You know it's not that! I've hired my managers, and I won't insult you by offering you a job as a waitress after all your experience."

"You'd better not. I might take it," she snapped back.

His fingers clenched the napkin. She had the impression he was making an effort to control his emotions, but if so, he wasn't successful. "Don't be ridiculous. What I was trying to say is that I'd be happy to make you a loan," he said sharply.

"It's a bit late to do me much good now. What I need is a job."

"A loan would tide you over for the short term. It would be a business loan, to be repaid when you sell. You can pay interest, if that relieves the aroma of accepting a favor." He was ill at ease making the offer, though he tried to sound businesslike. And she was not gratified to receive it.

Money was impersonal, the easiest way to be rid of her importunities. She didn't want money; she wanted work. She needed something to do, to fill her empty days, and she had been fool enough to think she might do that something in David's lodge, where she'd at least see him. Maybe that was why he was so determined not to have her there.

"I'm not reduced to begging. I could always take a

mortgage if it came to that," she answered stiffly. "Thanks anyway, David. Now, how about some of that cheesecake?" she asked heartily.

David leaped to terminate the touchy subject. "A good idea. I'm glad to see you've a good appetite." She noticed he was distressed—even gauche for him. He could see the pastrami sandwich on her plate, hardly touched. "You're looking better, too, I might add," he said, hoping to smooth over the interlude with a compliment.

"Better than what?" she asked. Her disappointment was already turning to anger. "Better than death, you mean?" she added with a piercing look.

He met her look without flinching. Something in his face held her gaze. It was the enigmatic expression that caught her interest—not happy, yet not angry like her either. Impatience was as close as she could come to describing it. "I'm damnably sorry about New York, Lisa. I behaved like an utter idiot. I wanted so much to see you, chased all over town after I received your message, and finally found you—with Lefty."

She opened her lips for a hot rejoinder, and David rushed on. "Marnie explained about him, that he's everyone's brother. Good old Lefty. Thank God he's going to California," he added with great feeling.

Lisa's feelings were taken on a roller coaster ride—a soar of hope, wavering to uncertainty, to be sidetracked to hearing Lefty was leaving. "California! You mean he's actually going through with it!" she exclaimed.

"He's leaving right away, I hear, but he'll probably be back."

Somehow the uncomfortable moment had passed. New York, the entire fiasco had been wiped out with a few words.

"Will you be back at the inn this afternoon for Nadia's visit?" David asked suddenly.

"No," she said curtly, even before asking at what time she meant to go. "Leo will show her around."

"I hope you'll be nice to her," he said. Such a strange thing to say. Why was he worried? The whole town would be nice to Mrs. Spencer. She wouldn't lack for friends. And why should she and Nadia ever meet again in their whole lives, if Nadia didn't plan to move here? It was a corroboration of her suspicion.

"I have nothing against her. She seemed very friendly," Lisa said through stiff lips.

"She's charming," he agreed enthusiastically. "Our families have been friends forever. Marnie was one of her better students, till she got bitten by the acting bug. I'm happy to say she's got that out of her system now and is doing some quite good work with Nadia. It wouldn't do her any harm to spend some time here in this neighborhood, and Nadia would certainly be a stabilizing influence on her." He stopped short, as though he had said more than he planned.

"I'll be nice to Marnie, too," she said with an ironic glance. "I really have to run now, David."

"But we haven't had our cheesecake!" he pointed out.

"At least we haven't ordered it. You stay and have yours. I'll run along." She began gathering up her purse to leave.

"I seem to have lost my appetite as well." He beckoned the waitress for the check, paid it, and they left.

When they were outside he asked if he could drop her somewhere, but she declined. "I have a little shopping to do. Thanks again. Say good-bye to Nadia for me. It was nice to meet her." The irony of that speech stuck in her throat.

"I'll let *you* tell her, next time we meet," he parried. There was a cryptic smile on his lips, and a light of amusement in his eyes. He immediately put on his sunglasses, as though fearful of betraying too much by his expression. She turned away and walked blindly down the street and escaped into the first shop she came to.

It was another restaurant, a small one with a bar. She ordered a cup of coffee to have an excuse to sit and nurse her wounds. If fate had any more blows in store for her, she'd hide. She'd find a hermitage and join it, lock herself away from the world and become a recluse. Life was too hard.

When she had her emotions under control, she glanced at her watch and noticed she had half an hour to kill. She walked slowly along to the bus terminal, bought a fashion magazine, and flipped through it while waiting for the bus. She heard the squealing of the brakes and walked out to join the small crowd waiting to board, thankful that it wouldn't be uncomfortably crowded. She was in no mood to talk to a stranger.

It was the slow bus, the one that left New York and stopped at every small town and village, sometimes even for an individual passenger waiting by the road in front of his house. The darkness inside made vision imperfect, but at least she could see which seats were unoccupied, and she wanted to sit alone if possible. She felt a tugging at her skirt as she walked past one seat and thought she'd got it hooked on something. She turned around to free it and saw the handsome face of Lefty Spinner smiling up at her.

"Hi, Boss Lady. Welcome aboard," he said, gallantly pointing to the empty seat beside him. "Long time, no see. I'm off to L.A. I'm stopping at the inn to pick up the rest of my stuff. My records and books and some clothes. You didn't throw them out?"

"No, they're in the attic. Lefty, it's good to see you again."

"Ditto."

"I hear *Tossed Salad* folded. Tough luck," she said with a sympathetic pat on his arm.

"It wilted," he agreed. "That's show biz. How's business?"

"My act is folding, too."

"Well, life's like a hotel in a way," he said resignedly.

"Dad used to say it was the world in miniature. You meet all kinds of people."

"I'm talking the *meaning* of life, Boss," he said, staring into her eyes. "I'm talking *your* hotel. You set yourself a goal, you struggle like hell for years, then you fall flat on your keyster. Story of my life, too. The story of more lives than you could number, Lisa Baby. You're not alone." He took her hand in his and squeezed it. Then he spoiled the whole gesture by offering her a stick of gum.

While he chewed, she filled him in on the details of what had been going on at the inn. She happened to mention that she'd had lunch with David, then added, "He's here with a woman named Nadia Milstrom. Did Marnie happen to mention her?"

"Does she ever mention anything else?" he asked. "Oh, yeah, Nadia is the new guru with the Spencer set. Old brother Dave is mighty taken with her. I haven't met her myself. Is she cute?" he asked with some interest.

"No, she's more . . . handsome," Lisa decided. "She's not young enough to be cute." She hadn't the heart to question Lefty further. All the evidence pointed the same way.

They talked till the bus stopped at the road in front of the inn. With Lefty to divert her, she forgot her intention of sneaking in to avoid Nadia. She entered the lobby, calling Leo to tell him Lefty was back.

"We're right here, Lisa," Leo said, coming out of the bar with Nadia beside him. She was dressed in a pale blue suit today, with a white straw hat swathed in navy veils. She looked very elegant, very citified.

"Lisa, nice to see you again." Nadia smiled, but soon her dark eyes were turning to Lefty. He was unkempt from the bus ride, and his hair had grown to an awkward length, but his topaz eyes were still excruciatingly bright, and his tanned face was handsome. His head began to wag as he surveyed Nadia.

"This is Lefty Spinner," Lisa said, and introduced them.

"I'm the social director at Paradise Inn," Lefty said, grasping Nadia's hand for a prolonged squeeze. "Ex, actually. I'm heading west—L.A."

"How nice," Nadia said, smiling. "Leo has been showing me around the gardens. Very sweet, the way you've set them up, Lisa. Ten acres in all, I think?" she asked with real interest.

"Yes, ten," Lisa told her. "Would you like a drink, Nadia?" she felt obliged to add as the woman waited with apparently no intention of leaving.

"Leo just gave me one, thank you. I really have to get back to town. I'm meeting David at four, and I . . . want to shower first and get into something comfortable. Warm for this time of year, isn't it?"

"I'll show you to your car, Nadia," Lefty said, then took her elbow in a close grip to accompany her out.

"Thank God I missed that," Lisa said to Leo when they were alone. "How long was she here?"

"She stayed from one till three. She's certainly interested in these old inns. It's a kind of hobby of hers, I believe. She's been to see the Cloverleaf on the other side of the mountain as well. I get the idea she's thinking of moving down here, she asked so many questions," he added in a considering way.

"Did she say anything specific?" Lisa inquired, her interest quickened at his speech.

"She just talked about the weather and the scenery, but in a very interested way. She said it would be lovely in the spring, and something about looking forward to seeing the mountain in the autumn, when the leaves are in color. Just a few little things. I gave a hint or two for curiosity's sake, and she said she thought it would be quaint to live in a quiet, bucolic spot like this," Leo told her. "I had a moment's wild hope we might have a buyer on our hands, but then a potter would hardly want to run an inn on the side."

"No, I don't believe that's what she has in mind," Lisa said, but she didn't state her own notions regarding Nadia Milstrom.

"So our Lefty is back," Leo said, shaking his head.

"It's just a stopover on his way west," Lisa said and told Leo his plans.

"That lad's a straw in the breeze. He doesn't know what he wants, but he knows he doesn't want to work," Leo complained.

"At least he's friendly."

"He likes to be liked, but he doesn't like to be loved, or depended on. There's the secret of Lefty Spinner, but I'll get him cleaning the windows all the same. We've got to keep the place polished up to look attractive to any lookers."

"I don't suppose the real estate people called while I was

out?'' Lisa asked. This was an inevitable question, even if
she only went out to the garden.

''No, they didn't,'' Leo told her sadly. ''But they will,
one of these days.''

True to his word, Leo gave Lefty a bottle of window
cleaner and a handful of rags and led him to the windows.
Leo and Lisa went to the kitchen, where Leo had a chicken
roasting, and made other preparations for dinner.

When they all sat down to eat, Lefty broached the subject
of Nadia. ''She's an attractive woman,'' he said. ''There's
money there, too. She mentioned a summer place at
Martha's Vineyard that she's got up for sale.''

''For sale, you say?'' Leo asked, with the small-town
man's quick interest in strangers. ''We were wondering if
she's thinking of moving here, to Spelling.''

''Same thing occurred to me,'' Lefty said, spearing a
chicken breast with his fork. ''Would you mind if I stick
around for a day or so, Boss Lady? The old inn needs my
special touch. Tomorrow I'll vacuum the pool for you, trim
the grass.''

It was extremely unlikely that either of these chores
would get done without the use of force, and virtually
certain that his staying on had to do with an interest in
Nadia.

''You're wasting your time,'' Lisa warned him. ''She's
taken.''

''I know when a lady's interested in Lefty,'' he told her.
She and Leo exchanged a resigned look and ate their
chicken.

Lefty was stacking the dishwasher and Lisa was tidying
the kitchen when Leo came in. ''The phone for you, Lisa,''
he said. ''I believe it's young Spencer.''

''Oh!'' Lisa exclaimed in a weak voice, and the cream

jug she was holding fell to the floor. "I'll take it at the switchboard."

One phrase had been running around in her head all day. "I wanted so much to see you," he had said. So it couldn't have been serious with Nadia and David then, a short month ago. But falling in love didn't require a month. She of all people knew that.

Chapter Eleven

Her hand was trembling when she picked up the receiver. In spite of her conjectures about Nadia and David, and in spite of all the evidence that seemed to corroborate it, a sprout of hope burst forth.

"Hello," she said, flinching when her voice broke, to betray her emotion.

"Lisa, how are you? I hope I didn't interrupt your dinner," David said. His voice betrayed nothing.

"No, you didn't. Is that David?" she asked, though she knew perfectly well it was, and the knowledge unnerved her.

"Yes, I was wondering if I could see you tonight, if you're not busy."

"Where? What for? I mean—what about Nadia?" she said, the words coming out in a quick jumble.

"There's some kind of an arts-and-crafts show on here in

town. She's gone over to it to meet the artisans. I have something I'd like to discuss with you—a business proposition," he added.

Her first wild hopes plummeted, but the intriguing "business proposition," hinting at a job offer, was some consolation. "Yes, of course I'll see you. What time will be convenient?" she asked.

"I can leave right now and be there in fifteen minutes. Is that all right?" he asked with adequate eagerness.

"That's fine. I'll see you then."

She hung up the phone and sat dazed for a moment. A business proposition, but at least he was coming, and without Nadia. She flew to the kitchen and told Leo and Lefty, then ran up to her room and began a major job on her appearance. She'd meet him at the door; they'd walk out in the garden as it was a beautiful evening. That way, Leo and Lefty wouldn't be around. They had first met in Ophelia's Garden. Would it stir up old memories for him, as it invariably did for her?

She'd wear something floaty and romantic. She scrambled out of her old clothes and into the dress she had meant to wear in New York. The flaring skirt brushed just below her knees. She slid into high-heeled sandals, splashed water on her face, and carefully applied a masking cream under her eyes. She put on mascara, a touch of blush on her cheeks, lipstick, the works. She brushed her Titian hair back to form a crown that glinted with lights in the reflection from the lamp, then surveyed herself. Her few stints at the pool had given her pale skin a becoming touch of color. She lightly sprayed a floral scent behind her ears and at her wrists, and went downstairs to wait.

Her heart sank when she saw Lefty lounging at the front desk. "All dressed up, eh, Boss Lady? Are you and Dave going to do the high spots of Spelling?'' he asked with the jaded scorn of a New Yorker.

"This is a business meeting," she answered briefly.

"So I see." He smiled knowingly. "You want me to take a hike, right?"

"You got it," she agreed.

"Never let it be said old Lefty stood in the way of romance. Break a leg, like we say in the theater," he added, then strolled off. "Oh, by the way," he called over his shoulder, "where's the van? Mind if I borrow it tonight?"

"It's gone. Why do you think I was on the bus?"

"No wheels! What a drag," he muttered, but at least he kept walking away. She was afraid he'd want to tell her about life being a broken-down jalopy.

She sat in state in the lounge, waiting for the sound of wheels on the road in front. *I hope he offers me a* good *job*, she thought, clenching her hands into fists. Hostess, receptionist, with the opportunity of advancement to management. But before the sound of wheels was finally heard, she admitted that the butterflies in her stomach weren't fluttering over the hope of a job. He couldn't be marrying Nadia. He *couldn't!* "I wanted so much to see you," he'd said. Then there was a tap at the door, and she rushed forth to greet him.

A startled smile lit his face when he saw her, all dressed up, with a flush of excitement brightening her cheeks, and a sparkle in her eyes. His dark eyes caressed her lingeringly. "I was picturing you in pink," he said and laughed.

"My pink days are over, and I'm half glad," she told him. "Do you want to come in, or shall we talk outside? It's such a lovely evening." Her tone suggested a mild indifference to place.

"Let's go out," he said at once. "Tonight that full moon

I promised you last summer is actually here, hanging like a pumpkin in the sky.'' He held the door wide and they went out into the black velvet night together.

This talk of moons didn't sound like business. She took heart when he placed his hand on her elbow and walked around to the rear of the inn, toward the pond and Ophelia's Garden.

"It *is* a lovely moon, isn't it?'' he asked, stopping by the pond. The moon was reflected in the water, a shimmering, irregular circle of cool fire. "Shall I dive in and fish it out for you?'' he suggested, whimsically cocking his head to the side.

"Shouldn't you have a platter standing by? The moon on a platter is the customary gift to . . . to a woman, isn't it?'' she asked, embarrassed at what had nearly slipped out. It wasn't just any woman who got the moon on a platter.

"I have something better—more practical anyway—to offer you,'' he said, inclining his head to hers till their noses nearly touched. He wore a beatific smile, like a man on the edge of declaring his love. No business had ever been conducted with such an attitude.

Her pulse throbbed in her throat at the nearness of him, in this private, enchanted spot. The dream had miraculously come true. He loved her, and now she was going to hear the words. Her body swayed toward his, drawn like a magnet, drinking in the vision of him, bathed in moonlight, with love reflected in his eyes.

"Make me an offer I can't refuse,'' she tempted, in a silken voice of invitation.

"I'm not actually in a position to offer, but I bring good tidings of great joy. Lisa, you'll never guess! Nadia wants to buy Paradise Inn,'' he announced joyfully.

She stepped back, the smile frozen in place, while she

took a closer look at David. She interpreted his mood differently now. He was just happy for a friend, that was all. It was his playful manner that had deluded her, led her mind astray.

"David, that's wonderful!" she managed to get out in a strangled voice.

"I couldn't be happier for you, Lisa," he said, and took her arm again to walk around the bank of the man-made lake. "I knew Nadia was looking for a headquarters for her new pottery works. She's very good, you know. She has a dozen or so students who want to work with her. These are graduate students from regular arts-and-crafts courses who want to go on and pick up a few of the more esoteric trade secrets," he explained.

"But why here? Why not in New York?" she asked.

"Nadia studied in Europe. I guess she wants to use the old apprenticeship method, with the students living with the master, or in this case mistress. Room, board, and tuition all rolled up into one expensive package. The inn suits her needs perfectly. I mentioned it to her when I saw the sign on your inn a while ago. I called you on that visit, but you were out," he said with a questioning look.

"Yes, I called back, but you'd left," she told him.

"Nadia's in a position to pay your asking price, so don't let her bargain you down too much. It will be a good deal for both of you. She'll have all the household things she needs—linens, dishes and so on—and you'll unload your cargo in one shot. She's fascinated by the location," he added enthusiastically, and continued with other details.

Lisa was delighted with the news, but a residue of disappointment remained with her. The visit *was* just business, when all was said and done.

"That was considerate of you to mention my place to

her,'' she said with real gratitude. ''I don't know how to thank you.''

''Use your imagination—that wonderfully *romantic* imagination of yours,'' he invited in a soft voice that sent a thrill of alarm through her.

She gave him a questioning look but didn't know quite how to respond to his suggestion. He didn't make any move to tighten his hold on her arm or to embrace her. After a moment's embarrassed pause, she said, ''I'm amazed she offered after the way I ran the place down.''

He quickly took her up on this. ''I was afraid you were going to botch it. Why the devil did you take it into your head to put the place down? Laughing at your decor, and checking off all the leaky roofs and sagging floors. That's the *buyer's* role.''

''How was I supposed to know she was a potential buyer? Why didn't you give me the clue?'' she countered.

''I wasn't sure she'd care for it, and didn't want to get your hopes up if nothing was going to come of it. You didn't need another disappointment, Lisa,'' he said, his voice turning gentle.

''I wonder what she likes about this corny place,'' she mentioned later, looking around at her little aids to romance —the Lovers' Lane, the Garden of Eden beyond.

''Corny! I thought you liked it!'' he objected, with almost an air of offense, as he peered down at her with shadowed eyes.

''You know perfectly well it's maudlin,'' she scoffed, though she still found considerable charm in it, bathed in moonlight as it was at this moment, and with David as an escort.

''You were more than halfway to convincing me otherwise,'' he said in a soft voice. She felt the brush of his fingers on her chin, turning her face back to him. She looked up to see him gazing at her with a bemused smile. "Romance is a little like religion. It looks strange only to those of another faith. We all believe in our own. I hope you haven't lost your faith in romance, Lisa," he said.

"Romance let me down," she said, a little trace of bitterness creeping into her voice. "I found I couldn't make a living at it."

"Perhaps your mistake was to try. Romance and commerce are not congenial, but it was a nice mistake. I admire you for the effort. You tried so hard to create an idyllic spot for young lovers, but in the end the numbers defeated you. You tried to give them too much for their money. Nadia won't be so unrealistic. She'll run a good business, but personally, I'll take romance."

His harsher features mirrored the wistful look Lisa wore. She thought of her shattered dream, her inn turned into a pottery workshop, and felt saddened. "I should tell Leo the good news," she said, trying for a smile. "Now he can have his hobby farm and play with his chickens and a cow. He's always wanted to do it."

"What are your plans, Lisa?" he asked as they strolled back to the front door.

"They're not firm. I can afford to take some time off to think now," she answered.

His hand that gripped her elbow slid down her arm till he was holding her fingers. She sensed some meaning in this seemingly casual motion, some heightened sensitivity in the very air around them. "I hope you're not thinking of moving away, or anything major like that, are you?" he asked, leaning down to look at her face, a pale oval in the moonlight.

"My mind is floating free," she said as the truth of her

position began to sink in. "I don't put anything beyond possibility. I might even take a half year off and go to Europe. I've always wanted to do it," she said, and listened hopefully for a roar of objection to this plan.

"Europe is a wonderful idea!" he said at once. "You've earned a good rest. Don't you think two months would be long enough, though?" he added with a frown. "There are large pockets of Europe hardly worth a visit."

"No, I don't want to miss anything. I might even stay a year," she said recklessly. Why bother to come back at all if he was so happy to see her go?

"Don't be so foolish!" he said angrily.

"I've earned the right to a little folly," she insisted. "It'll be the first time in my life that I've been free of financial obligations."

"There are other kinds of obligations," he pointed out with a notable air of offense.

"Oh, I'll take care of them, too, if you're referring to Leo and my employees," she replied, her voice mischievously innocent.

"That was *not* the obligation I referred to, as you very well know."

Emboldened by this response, she tilted a coquettish smile at him. "Are you hinting for a finder's fee? What percent are *you* planning to gouge me for?"

"One hundred percent," he said, his fingers gripping hers tightly. "And I'm *not* talking money."

As they approached the front door, Lefty chose that inopportune moment to come out. "Hi, guys. Can I bum a ride to town with you when you go, Dave?" he asked cheerfully.

David muttered something beneath his breath, and with a scowl answered, "I suppose so."

"Great. Are we leaving now? I'll have to catch the midnight bus back. I want to have a few hours in town." As he spoke, he came forward and positioned himself between Lisa and David.

"Why don't you go and get your jacket and meet me at the car?" David suggested, hoping to get rid of him.

"Not to worry. I don't need a jacket," Lefty said and stood waiting.

David stepped around him and faced Lisa. "A year is out of the question," he said sternly. "One month is more than adequate." Then he turned to Lefty, scowled again, and stalked off to the car.

Lisa suppressed the urge to commit homicide on Lefty Spinner, then went to tell Leo the news instead.

Chapter Twelve

Nadia came with the real estate agent the next day and took a leisurely tour of the whole premises. An hour after they left, the agent returned with a formal offer to purchase. Lisa and Leo discussed it for a few moments in private, but the price was good, and a firm, unconditional offer was hard to resist. Lisa didn't know whether she was glad or sorry when she wrote her name with shaking fingers on the dotted line. There, it was done. She had signed away her patrimony, and on November 15 she would be the holder of more money than she had ever dared to hope for.

The closing date in mid-November seemed rather long to wait, but Leo thought Miss Milstrom must have business to terminate in New York. It kept them bound to Paradise Inn till that time, as no monies would be received till that date. Two days later Nadia came to the inn with some of her students to select the best area for her work and classes. The potters' wheels and the kiln had to be installed.

"I wish we could get an earlier start, but my first class doesn't begin till the new year, so six weeks should do it," Nadia said, chatting to Lisa afterward.

"Will the school run year round?" Lisa asked.

"No, no. Just from September to the end of April. I need some time to myself, to do my own work uninterrupted. It will be rather lonesome rattling around this huge place all alone," she added.

"May to September was always the busiest time here before," Lisa said, smiling wistfully at her collection of memories.

"Yes, the wedding season," Nadia said. "It's a pity to have the inn standing idle . . ." She stopped, and for a moment the two women looked at each other. Later, they couldn't agree which of them had come up with the idea. Nadia claimed it for her own, but Lisa secretly disagreed.

In any case, it was Lisa who said, "Actually, there's no reason you couldn't run both your school, *and* the honeymoon inn during the summer."

"But where would I have the pottery workshop?"

"You could have the courtyard turned into one."

"It would be much easier to build a studio from scratch than to convert the dance hall, which was my original intention," Nadia said, warming to the scheme. "But I wouldn't have either the time or knowledge to run the place. I'd have to hire a manager."

"I'm sure Leo would stay on long enough for you to train him," Lisa suggested. Strangely, she didn't want to put herself forward for the job. She'd cut the umbilical cord, finished with that part of her life. It demanded too much from her, and while she'd been willing to give it her all when it was her own place, she didn't want to do it for anyone else. She'd no longer be in complete control, and she was too used to that.

"I'm just *itching* to get at it," Nadia said, her face even more vibrant than usual. "Why did you want such a late closing date, Lisa? Isn't there any way we could close the deal sooner?"

"I beg your pardon?" Lisa asked, bewildered. *"You* were the one who suggested mid-November—it was on your offer to purchase."

"But David told me that's what you wanted. *He* said an early closing date would be very inconvenient for you," Nadia said with a questioning look. "I wanted to move as soon as possible."

David had done Lisa a big favor, and Lisa was grateful to him, but that was no reason to inconvenience both Nadia and herself. "It must have been a misunderstanding," she said.

"It probably was. He's so preoccupied with his own business that he got the dates mixed up. It's the ski lodge that opens officially in mid-November, of course. That's what he had on his mind. Why don't we speak to the agent and change the date, if you have no objection?" Nadia urged.

"It suits me fine," Lisa agreed.

The arrangement was made formal that same day with the agent. Throughout the rest of September, Nadia frequently came to Spelling to visit the inn, often bringing loads of her possessions with her. Lisa invited her to sleep at the inn during these visits for convenience's sake. She also enjoyed her company, now that she had no paying guests.

Lefty was sure to be around when Nadia was there. It became a common sight to see Lefty or Leo poking around the premises with Nadia. Leo had agreed to remain on as manager of the honeymoon hotel in the summer, and Nadia was at work to keep him there year-round as general factotum.

"No one knows as much about the idiosyncracies of the septic tank and well water as you, Leo," she said guilefully. "All those horrid pumps and plumbing things are beyond me. Are you irrevocably decided to buy yourself a few acres and turn farmer?"

"Well, I haven't had much luck finding a small farm that suits me," he admitted. "And I find I'm not so fond of my own cooking as I thought I'd be either."

"Then you'll stay!" Nadia beamed.

"For the time being, but I'm not as young as I once was," he cautioned her.

"Not by a long shot," Lefty agreed. "What you need is a *young* man to do the physical labor. Pool, windows, a ton of snow to shovel in the winter, all those bags of clay to haul around." He flexed his impressive muscles as he spoke.

"Of course, I'll need more than one man around the place," Nadia said with an assessing look at Lefty. "Leo won't do the heavy work."

"I accept. Glad to help you out," Lefty decided unilaterally. "I'll be Leo's assistant manager till he retires. Mind you, I can't promise I'll take over as manager when he goes. Life's a winding road. Who knows what's around the next bend?" Nadia felt fairly sure the manager's chair wasn't around the bend for Lefty, but she let him keep his illusions. A good manager wouldn't be hard to find. "I must warn you, come winter I'll be available only part-time. I plan to do some instructing at the new ski lodge. Always wanted to be a ski bum."

"Has young Spencer hired you?" Leo asked in surprise.

"Not yet," Lefty admitted, unashamed. "I haven't had time to mention it to him."

"I didn't know you could ski," Lisa said.

"Nothing to it. I'll learn in no time, and meanwhile I can fake it," Lefty told her with his usual excess of confidence. "Life's a ski hill, when you come to think of it. Start at the top, take a few tumbles along the way, and first thing you know, there you are at the bottom. Sounds like my life anyway," he added with a rare bit of insight.

"What about L.A.?" Lisa asked, her lips unsteady.

"Hate California. It's cold and it's damp," he told her. With his head beginning to wag, he turned his beautiful eyes to Nadia. "Many chicks enrolled in your school, Boss Lady?"

Lisa noted that the mantle of power had passed from her shoulders. "It's mostly women actually," Nadia informed him. "And they're all strictly off limits to the hired help," she added firmly.

"Naturally!" Lefty exclaimed, grossly offended at the imputation of girl chasing.

Everyone was settled except Lisa. Nadia returned to New York that evening, leaving the three others alone at the inn.

"What will you do after the sale, Lisa? I hope you won't move too far away," Leo said.

"Why don't you stay here, too, Lisa?" Lefty suggested.

":I don't have your knack of landing a job, Lefty. Besides, I'm not particularly interested in pottery," she replied.

"Not interested in pottery?" he asked, outraged. "Where would we be without pottery? What would we drink out of, and eat off of, and stick on our tables and shelves to look pretty? What would we do with all that clay?"

She didn't argue, but decided to leave the room, before he told her life was just a potter's wheel, or a handful of clay. She went up to her apartment to pack her personal belongings.

It was much later when her phone rang, indicating that someone had transferred a call from the downstairs switchboard. A telephone call always sent her into a spasm of hope that it would be David, but at ten o'clock at night she didn't think it at all likely. It would only be Leo, asking her if she wanted a sandwich or a cup of tea.

"Lisa, it's David," she heard, with a thrill of joy.

She hadn't seen him, hadn't heard from him since the night he had come to tell her Nadia wanted to buy her inn. She realized from chance remarks made by Nadia that she and David were only friends, but a friend was all he was to her, too.

"David, are you in Spelling?" she asked eagerly, her fingers clutching the phone.

"No, I'm in New York. Nadia just gave me a call. What's this about moving up the date of sale on the inn?" he asked, his voice betraying agitation.

"Yes, we did. She wanted to move in sooner, and I had no objection. Why did you suggest a November closing date to her?" she asked, but he completely ignored the question.

"That's rushing things a bit, isn't it?" he asked.

"Not really. She's going to keep Lefty and Leo on, so there's no problem there," she explained.

"I know, but what about *you?*" he asked quickly.

"Don't worry about me," she said airily. "With all that money in my hot little hands, I'll be all right." She held her breath to hear his reply.

"I'm coming down to Spelling tonight," he said. There was a desperate note in his voice.

"Tonight? David, it's ten o'clock! You wouldn't be here till all hours. What—why . . ." She swallowed nervously, trying to phrase her question in an unassuming manner.

"You're right. I'd better wait till morning," he agreed, but with some doubt. "If I left at dawn tomorrow, I'd be there by mid-morning."

Lisa heard this with a sense of disappointment, but said nothing.

After a short silence, David spoke again in a different, a firmer voice. "No, I won't sleep anyway. I'm leaving now. You pop into bed and get a few hours' sleep, and be prepared for a pelting of stones on your window between two and three in the morning," he said.

A sense of excitement invaded her at his eager plan. "Don't be an idiot," she said, a soft smile curving her lips.

"Why change my ways now? The idiot will be there. Maybe sooner than you think!" he added in a mischievous voice, then hung up.

She gently replaced the receiver and sat alone, just smiling at it. He was coming. Now, tonight. Driving all those tiresome miles in the middle of the night to see her. She felt a frisson of fear that he might drive too fast and have an accident. His suggestion that she go to bed was totally ignored.

A woman didn't go to bed and sleep when she was in imminent hope of receiving a proposal. Why else was he dashing through the night to see her? What other reason would put that edge of recklessness on his behavior? One hundred percent he meant to claim, and she was ready to give herself to him entirely. She lay down and allowed her thoughts to roam over her bright future.

What a conniver the man was. From the first time she'd

laid eyes on him, he'd been misleading her. He had told
Nadia to delay the closing of purchase on the inn to
November so that the ski lodge would be open, and he
would be here. He didn't want her to go off to Europe, and
had used that ruse to keep her tied down. No money, no
trip. She felt not a shadow of censure at such underhanded
tactics.

Her energy level was suddenly too high to allow her to
remain on the bed. She rose and went out to Juliet's balcony
to dream by the light of the fat orange moon. There was a
chill breeze in the air, and she pulled the lace-edged runner
from the dresser to drape around her shoulders. Occasionally she glanced at her watch. How had it got to be midnight
already? David would be halfway here. He'd be looking at
his watch, too, thinking of her. She felt she was with him in
spirit.

Her pleasant reverie was interrupted by the harsh whir-
ring of a helicopter. She watched it pass in silhouette
against the moon, incongruous in the romantic moonlight.
What could a helicopter be doing here so late at night? She
watched as it began to descend, just past the boundary of
her land, in a farmer's field. Was it an emergency? It didn't
look like a compulsory landing. The vehicle settled gently
to earth beyond the treeline. Such an unusual occurrence
might have aroused more curiosity at another time, but
tonight it was only an oddity, forgotten as soon as the
helicopter swooped into the sky again a moment later, and
disappeared.

When the dark shadow of a man emerged silently from
the bowed arch of Lovers' Lane, Lisa was moonraking. She
didn't see David till he stood below the balcony, gazing up
at her, his face bathed in wan moonlight.

"David!" she exclaimed then, mystified at the apparition. Had she fallen asleep? Was it mid-morning already? The moon and the black velvet sky denied it.

She watched in happy perplexity as he grasped the trunk of the climbing vine and pulled himself up. His fingers grabbed the floor of the balcony, and with a few faint, scrabbling sounds, he was suddenly there beside her.

"Where did you come from?" she gasped, almost frightened at this inexplicable apparition.

"From the sky, your own personal *deus ex machina*." He smiled. "It happens in all the best Greek dramas."

"The helicopter! It was *you!*" she exclaimed.

"I was never a helicopter, only a very impatient passenger. Lisa, why did you do it?" he demanded, his arms already around her.

"What—change the closing date?" she asked breathlessly. "Nadia didn't want to wait so long," she said, her arms looping around his neck while she leaned back against his arms to observe him.

"*Nadia* didn't want to wait! Who did? Do you think *I* relished the thought of sitting on my thumbs for a whole six weeks till I had a few minutes free, and a home at the lodge to take you to?" he asked, in a voice that felt justified in being angry, but was unable to hold its tone. His voice softened as he gazed down at her from those inky eyes, shadowed with dark lashes.

"Why didn't you say anything to me?" she asked, her lips trembling petulantly.

"I didn't care for the scenario, as our friend Lefty would say. The great white savior Spencer arranging your life, the sale of your inn, with the little corollary slipped in, and 'Oh, yes, by the way, you'll marry me, of course.' When—*if* you marry me, Lisa, don't do it for gratitude. I arranged the sale for *me*. I didn't want to ask you when you were in desperate need of money, and worried about your future. No pressures, but only because you *want* to, as I want to marry you,'' he said in a husky voice.

Her heart jerked at the words. He stopped and waited, staring as though mesmerized at the eyes that gazed back at him, wide and unblinking.

"If you'd offered me a job, I wouldn't have been desperate," she pointed out dutifully.

"No favors, no gratitude. Just because you want to, Lisa," he repeated softly. "You're independent now. Do you want to marry me? I'll *try* not to tilt you over the balcony if you say no," he added with mock menace, glancing over the railing.

"Idiot! I always wanted to marry you," she said on a gurgling laugh of exultant joy. It was stifled by a kiss as his lips possessed hers. His arms cradled her against him, swaying in an hypnotic rhythm, lulled by the rays of the benign moon.

"You had a strange way of showing it," he said later, with her head nestled against his shoulder, while his hands warmed her back.

"A strange way of trying to conceal it, you mean," she countered. "How could I show a married man I loved him?"

"Like this," he said reasonably, tilting her face up to meet his. Their lips brushed and clung together in a searing kiss that annihilated logic and reason. She felt one with David, with the night breezes that blew on them, with the stars and moon. One with nature and the elements, a part of the vital force of life. Her very being throbbed with the joy of loving and being loved.

When their lips parted on a sigh, her eyes drifted open to

a dim view of the gardens that stretched away below the balcony.

"Are you sorry to be losing Paradise Inn?" he asked gently, following the path of her gaze.

"Oh, no, it will go on without me," she sighed happily. "Paradise isn't a place so much as a state of mind."

"And a state of heart," he added. "Mine feels as full and glowing as that moon." They turned together to gaze at it, smiling fondly at their secret thoughts.

There were details to be discussed later. But these trifles were forgotten now. It was a moment snatched from eternity, to be felt, enjoyed, unhampered by the trivia of mundane reality. They embraced again, with spirits soaring in the fulfillment of love, all unaware of the entrancing picture they made for Lefty and Leo, who had gone looking after the helicopter.

Leo smiled with infinite satisfaction, and Lefty cocked his head to the side. "Ain't love grand?" he asked with a world-weary smile. "Life's an embrace when you stop to think about it. A man, a woman—that's what started all the trouble in paradise."

Silhouette Romance

IT'S YOUR OWN SPECIAL TIME
Contemporary romances for today's women.
Each month, six very special love stories will be yours
from SILHOUETTE.

$1.75 each

☐ 100 Stanford	☐ 128 Hampson	☐ 157 Vitek	☐ 185 Hampson
☐ 101 Hardy	☐ 129 Converse	☐ 158 Reynolds	☐ 186 Howard
☐ 102 Hastings	☐ 130 Hardy	☐ 159 Tracy	☐ 187 Scott
☐ 103 Cork	☐ 131 Stanford	☐ 160 Hampson	☐ 188 Cork
☐ 104 Vitek	☐ 132 Wisdom	☐ 161 Trent	☐ 189 Stephens
☐ 105 Eden	☐ 133 Rowe	☐ 162 Ashby	☐ 190 Hampson
☐ 106 Dailey	☐ 134 Charles	☐ 163 Roberts	☐ 191 Browning
☐ 107 Bright	☐ 135 Logan	☐ 164 Browning	☐ 192 John
☐ 108 Hampson	☐ 136 Hampson	☐ 165 Young	☐ 193 Trent
☐ 109 Vernon	☐ 137 Hunter	☐ 166 Wisdom	☐ 194 Barry
☐ 110 Trent	☐ 138 Wilson	☐ 167 Hunter	☐ 195 Dailey
☐ 111 South	☐ 139 Vitek	☐ 168 Carr	☐ 196 Hampson
☐ 112 Stanford	☐ 140 Erskine	☐ 169 Scott	☐ 197 Summers
☐ 113 Browning	☐ 142 Browning	☐ 170 Ripy	☐ 198 Hunter
☐ 114 Michaels	☐ 143 Roberts	☐ 171 Hill	☐ 199 Roberts
☐ 115 John	☐ 144 Goforth	☐ 172 Browning	☐ 200 Lloyd
☐ 116 Lindley	☐ 145 Hope	☐ 173 Camp	☐ 201 Starr
☐ 117 Scott	☐ 146 Michaels	☐ 174 Sinclair	☐ 202 Hampson
☐ 118 Dailey	☐ 147 Hampson	☐ 175 Jarrett	☐ 203 Browning
☐ 119 Hampson	☐ 148 Cork	☐ 176 Vitek	☐ 204 Carroll
☐ 120 Carroll	☐ 149 Saunders	☐ 177 Dailey	☐ 205 Maxam
☐ 121 Langan	☐ 150 Major	☐ 178 Hampson	☐ 206 Manning
☐ 122 Scofield	☐ 151 Hampson	☐ 179 Beckman	☐ 207 Windham
☐ 123 Sinclair	☐ 152 Halston	☐ 180 Roberts	☐ 208 Halston
☐ 124 Beckman	☐ 153 Dailey	☐ 181 Terrill	☐ 209 LaDame
☐ 125 Bright	☐ 154 Beckman	☐ 182 Clay	☐ 210 Eden
☐ 126 St. George	☐ 155 Hampson	☐ 183 Stanley	☐ 211 Walters
☐ 127 Roberts	☐ 156 Sawyer	☐ 184 Hardy	☐ 212 Young

$1.95 each

☐ 213 Dailey	☐ 217 Vitek	☐ 221 Browning	☐ 225 St. George
☐ 214 Hampson	☐ 218 Hunter	☐ 222 Carroll	☐ 226 Hampson
☐ 215 Roberts	☐ 219 Cork	☐ 223 Summers	☐ 227 Beckman
☐ 216 Saunders	☐ 220 Hampson	☐ 224 Langan	☐ 228 King

Silhouette Romance

$1.95 each

☐ 229 Thornton	☐ 253 James	☐ 277 Wilson	☐ 301 Palmer
☐ 230 Stevens	☐ 254 Palmer	☐ 278 Hunter	☐ 302 Smith
☐ 231 Dailey	☐ 255 Smith	☐ 279 Ashby	☐ 303 Langan
☐ 232 Hampson	☐ 256 Hampson	☐ 280 Roberts	☐ 304 Cork
☐ 233 Vernon	☐ 257 Hunter	☐ 281 Lovan	☐ 305 Browning
☐ 234 Smith	☐ 258 Ashby	☐ 282 Halldorson	☐ 306 Gordon
☐ 235 James	☐ 259 English	☐ 283 Payne	☐ 307 Wildman
☐ 236 Maxam	☐ 260 Martin	☐ 284 Young	☐ 308 Young
☐ 237 Wilson	☐ 261 Saunders	☐ 285 Gray	☐ 309 Hardy
☐ 238 Cork	☐ 262 John	☐ 286 Cork	☐ 310 Hunter
☐ 239 McKay	☐ 263 Wilson	☐ 287 Joyce	☐ 311 Gray
☐ 240 Hunter	☐ 264 Vine	☐ 288 Smith	☐ 312 Vernon
☐ 241 Wisdom	☐ 265 Adams	☐ 289 Saunders	☐ 313 Rainville
☐ 242 Brooke	☐ 266 Trent	☐ 290 Hunter	☐ 314 Palmer
☐ 243 Saunders	☐ 267 Chase	☐ 291 McKay	☐ 315 Smith
☐ 244 Sinclair	☐ 268 Hunter	☐ 292 Browning	
☐ 245 Trent	☐ 269 Smith	☐ 293 Morgan	
☐ 246 Carroll	☐ 270 Camp	☐ 294 Cockcroft	
☐ 247 Halldorson	☐ 271 Allison	☐ 295 Vernon	
☐ 248 St. George	☐ 272 Forrest	☐ 296 Paige	
☐ 249 Scofield	☐ 273 Beckman	☐ 297 Young	
☐ 250 Hampson	☐ 274 Roberts	☐ 298 Hunter	
☐ 251 Wilson	☐ 275 Browning	☐ 299 Roberts	
☐ 252 Roberts	☐ 276 Vernon	☐ 300 Stephens	

SILHOUETTE BOOKS, Department SB/1
1230 Avenue of the Americas
New York, NY 10020

Please send me the books I have checked above. I am enclosing $_____
(please add 75¢ to cover postage and handling. NYS and NYC residents please
add appropriate sales tax). Send check or money order—no cash or C.O.D.'s
please. Allow six weeks for delivery.

NAME _____

ADDRESS _____

CITY _____ STATE/ZIP _____

MAIL THIS COUPON
and get 4 thrilling

Silhouette Desire®

novels FREE (a $7.80 value)

Silhouette Desire books may not be for everyone. They *are* for readers who want a sensual, provocative romance. These are modern love stories that are charged with emotion from the first page to the thrilling happy ending—about women who discover the extremes of fiery passion. Confident women who face the challenge of today's world and overcome all obstacles to attain their dreams—*and their desires.*

We believe you'll be so delighted with Silhouette Desire romance novels that you'll want to receive them regularly through our home subscription service. Your books will be *shipped to you two months before they're available anywhere else*—so you'll never miss a new title. Each month we'll send you 6 new books to look over for 15 days, without obligation. If not delighted, simply return them and owe nothing. Or keep them and pay only $1.95 each. There's no charge for postage or handling. And there's no obligation to buy anything at any time. You'll also receive a subscription to the Silhouette Books Newsletter *absolutely free!*

So don't wait. To receive your four FREE books, fill out and mail the coupon below *today!*

SILHOUETTE DESIRE and colophon are registered trademarks and a service mark of Simon & Schuster, Inc.

Silhouette Desire,® 120 Brighton Road, P.O. Box 5020, Clifton, NJ 07015

Yes, please send me FREE and without obligation, 4 exciting Silhouette Desire books. Unless you hear from me after I receive them, send me 6 new Silhouette Desire books to preview each month before they're available anywhere else. I understand that you will bill me just $1.95 each for a total of $11.70—with no additional shipping, handling or other hidden charges. **There is no minimum number of books that I must buy, and I can cancel anytime I wish.** The first 4 books are mine to keep, even if I never take a single additional book.

☐ Mrs. ☐ Miss ☐ Ms. ☐ Mr.   **BDR8R4**

Name	*(please print)*

Address	Apt. #

City	State	Zip

( )	
Area Code	Telephone Number

Signature (If under 18, parent or guardian must sign.)

This offer, limited to one per household, expires February 28, 1985. Terms and prices are subject to change. Your enrollment is subject to acceptance by Simon & Schuster Enterprises.